*W*ords of Praise for *the Forger's Key*

"Wendy VanHatten's latest addition to her Hidden Truths series, *The Forger's Key,* number five in the series, is her best yet in my opinion. Each of her offerings gets better and better. The writing is more refined, the story is smoother flowing, and it is always engaging. In fact, they are all hard to put down, keeping one moving along without tiring or losing interest.

"Marta, Clark, Ian, and the gang are back with some new characters. Loved the newspaper gal who was pure fun and spunk, and maybe, just maybe, someone else got into her car instead of Maxine . . . just so I can enjoy her again in the next installment! More romance seems likely too after all the intrigue cools at bit. I thoroughly enjoyed reading them all, but this one is best so far."

Terry Minion

"Marta, the main character in these novels, is at it again with her traveling, her cat, and her problems. Not to mention the bad guys who keep following her. I'm not sure how she can be so clueless and yet so lucky, but that's why I love her.

"There's enough suspense and twists to keep readers engaged in the action and with the characters. I really wasn't sure how this one was going to end . . . until it did."

Bev M

the Forger's Key

Hidden Truths Vol. 5

the Forger's Key

Wendy VanHatten

DocUmeant *Publishing*
244 5th Avenue
Suite G-200
NY, NY 10001
646-233-4366
www.DocUmeantPublishing.com

The Forger's Key

Hidden Truths Series, Vol. 5

Published byDocUmeant Publishing 244 5th Avenue, Suite G-200 NY, NY 10001

Phone: 646-233-4366

Copy Editor JoAnn Rasmussen

Cover Design and Layout Ginger Marks

DocUmeantDesigns.com

Printed in The United States of America

ISBN13: 978-1-937801-75-5 (14.99 USD)
ISBN10: 1-937801-75-6

Dedication

To Rick, who encourages me to keep writing.

$\mathscr{P}$rologue

IN LESS THAN three days, Marta's visit to Milan had turned from fun to dangerous, if she paid attention to Ian's unspoken words.

When he told her to be careful, and mentioned some issues surrounding forgeries Interpol was investigating, he looked right at her. Then, he told her to be careful. Again.

"Yep. Something's up. I'm still having a hard time believing that painting was a forgery. It looked so good. And, if someone went to all the trouble to hang a forgery, especially in that gallery, why would they mess up and use that frame? It just doesn't make sense. Maybe it's all just a mistake." Marta sighed. "Yeah, right." She shook her head. "Wishful thinking."

Yesterday morning, Marta's visit to a little museum gallery in Milan had turned into a big deal when she thought she spotted something odd about the frame of a particular painting. She couldn't put her finger on it, but it wasn't right. That's all she knew, and she called her best friend and art expert, Clark. Sure enough, when Clark involved Ian from Interpol, and he came to the museum, they discovered the painting was a forgery. Apparently, it was quite a spectacular forgery, but in a 20th century frame. That's what was bothering her. The frame had looked so modern; too perfect for an old painting.

If that wasn't enough, last night at dinner in an upscale restaurant in the Galleria, she was first confused and then alarmed when she saw a strange man snooping around her table, like he was looking for something. She was on her way back from the restroom, but before she could reach him, he abruptly fled the restaurant, knocking over a chair on his way out. She mentioned him to the maître d', but he had been extra busy and couldn't really remember him.

Ian's warnings stuck in her head as she made her way to the train station; the spoken ones and the unspoken ones.

Chapter 1

"DAMN IT." MARTA exited the cab and caught a glimpse of a man two cars behind her. She turned and watched as he quickly disappeared through the doors to the station. "Who the hell is that guy and what is he doing here? Is he following me?" She shivered.

The cab driver gave her a quizzical look as he closed the door. "Are you okay, Miss?"

"Sorry. I'm just talking to myself about a guy I think is following me, and I'm a little spooked."

He nodded as he handed her the small travel bag. "If you mean the one back there a couple of cabs, wearing the nice looking, dark green jacket, he left the hotel right after we did. He was standing outside and took the cab after mine. But, we bring a lot of people here. Will you be okay?"

"Yes. I'll be fine. And, I'm sure you're right. It's probably just a coincidence. Thanks again." She paid the driver and turned toward the station. She had caught a cab from her hotel near the Galleria Vittorio Emanuele II and was now at the Milan train station, waiting to go back to Venice. When she exited the cab, she happened to see a man; the same man who she first spotted glaring at her over his newspaper at breakfast, not more than 45 minutes ago.

1

That could have been a coincidence if she hadn't seen him again as she checked out of her hotel. He was standing by the doorway, watching, looking right at her. Now he was at the train station; three cabs behind her. "Damn it. He is following me. But, why? Is it the painting?"

Ian's warnings echoed loud and clear.

As she made her way through the elegant station, to the short line of people waiting to purchase tickets, she watched everyone, looking specifically for him. The polished windows, sparkling chandeliers, high, curved glass ceiling, exquisite shops, and designer boutiques didn't grab her attention like they usually did. She was only looking for one man. "Where the hell did he go?"

Once, she thought she saw him at a ticket window across from the grand, marble staircase, but when she looked closer, he wasn't there. Sighing, she realized there were too many people and not enough time for her to keep looking. After checking the departure schedule, she made her way to the platform for the train to Venice, and sent a quick text to Clark. "Saw the same man, at least twice. I know I'm not imagining it. He even had on the same jacket. I wonder if he has something to do with that painting? Any idea why he'd be following me?"

Now, as Marta settled in to her comfortable seat on the train, she accepted the glass of Prosecco from the attendant. She fully intended to work at least part of the two-hour trip. But, she was still a little on edge from the past two days, and her gut instinct was working overtime.

Talking softly to herself, she looked around once more. "Get a grip, Marta. Everyone here looks like a genuine tourist or businessman on their way to Venice. These events can't be connected to anything from last year, and anyway, I can't wait to get home and see Shadow, who will scold me for leaving him alone for four days. His cat sitter spoils him, but he'll still have plenty to meow about." She pulled her calendar out of her bag and started making notes, putting her paranoia aside.

Sitting at the far end of the same car, a man pulled his phone out of his dark green, tailored, suit coat pocket and sent a text.

"Boss, I've got the blonde in sight and will follow her to Venice. She hasn't noticed me. Awaiting your instructions."

$\mathcal{C}$hapter 2

HUNDREDS OF PERFECTLY round bubbles rose and fell as they danced in his glass. The half-empty bottle lounged in a silver ice bucket, just within his reach. San Francisco Bay and the Golden Gate Bridge provided the perfect backdrop as the setting sun changed the sky from indigo to amethyst to fuchsia before it slid into the Pacific Ocean. The air turned chilly on his arms and face as the night mist started to creep around him.

He noticed none of this.

He was deeply ensconced in his rage; a rage which caused the veins in his hands to bulge as he clenched the arms of his overstuffed, leather chair and the veins in his head to bulge, almost to the point of exploding all over the pristine patio. To say he was mad would be like comparing a charging bull elephant to a skittering cockroach. He was beyond mad; he was infuriated.

Images floated into his addled brain, and then out. With each one, his anger became more intense, his memories more vivid, and his plans more twisted. Bizarre thoughts and even more bizarre ideas free-flowed as his anger surged.

That bitch who called herself Mother deserved what she got; the bomb sure took care of her. Glad the clueless auctioneer got dumped. No sense dragging that out. Now, that so-called Italian artist who is trying to cheat me must be reminded who the boss is. Can't have

Dixie find out about that. And, I have plans to get rid of the little twit who calls herself an expert. She's just a nuisance; a fly to be swatted.

He flicked his hand into the air and poured another glass, spilling some onto the patio floor. Then, his mind focused on one more who caused him suffering, possibly incurring the wrath of Dixie. He spoke to no one, gesturing with his overflowing crystal flute.

"Damn, that meddling blonde.

"Right here in San Francisco she stuck her nose where it didn't belong and ultimately cost me my Picasso. What the hell was she doing messing around here? That Picasso forgery was ready to replace the original. Until they let that stupid twit bid on it, and she sold it to that clueless old couple. The original should be hanging in my den right now. The museum wouldn't have even known they had been switched. But, nooo, that didn't happen. What was that auctioneer thinking, anyway? He wasn't supposed to let anybody have it except my guy. Too late to think about him. He's at the bottom of the ocean and won't be selling anything there. Still, the dumb blonde had her fingers in that fiasco. Why?

"Then, she involved Interpol in Milan, and they discovered that forgery much too quickly. I still don't know how she knew what she was looking at. Now, Interpol thinks they know my name and what I look like. But, they don't. I'm much too careful for that. Still, she caused me to discard a perfectly good passport and identity. Worse, that same dumb blonde cost me a bundle there. Dixie is pressing me for answers on that one, and I don't like it. Damn woman thinks she can boss me around, too, like one of her thugs." His thoughts returned to the blonde.

"The blonde's definitely a liability. She has to be eliminated."

Shaking his head as if to clear the cobwebs, he drained the remaining champagne in his glass, and looked around. "I'll see to it the blonde won't live to do any more damage." He clasped and unclasped his hands as he looked at the empty patio, his frown deepening. His veins bulged to another level as he mumbled to himself. "Yes. She must be dealt with. Sooner than later. At least my guy is trailing her to Venice, so first he'll rough her up. Then, I'll figure out how to make her disappear."

His brow furrowed as once again his fingers dug into the arms of his chair. He sat this way, not moving a muscle, for several long minutes. Inside his brain, the pounding had increased. Slowly, his head came up, and his frown turned to a smirk as he stared into the dark. He refilled his glass and took another gulp of champagne as he spoke to the darkened patio, his madness and his headache surging to another level.

"First, I want them to know the end is near. They all deserve to be scared. They have no idea who they're messing with. It's time everybody knows who the real boss is. I'll call and put some fear into the no-good artist, and then I'll send Carlo to take care of him. Now, for the foolproof plan to get rid of both the blonde and her little friend." His bravado was building with each sip. "It would be perfect if they had the same unfortunate accident. Ha! I know. Boom! I do love it when things blow up." He stared into the dark, thinking, smiling, and rubbing his temples as his rambling increased and he became less coherent each passing minute.

Staring off into the now darkened sky, his smirk turned evil. "This is brilliant. I am brilliant. Easy. Easier than that stupid lady who called herself my mother. Hah. Nothing to it. I love planning this stuff."

He finished the champagne and made his first phone call, which went right to voicemail, and that made him madder than he had been all night. Well, almost. Clenching his phone in his hand, he left a caustic message.

"Since you're in deep trouble with me right now, you'd better have a good reason for not answering your phone. I assume you're there and just too busy working on something for me to take time to answer. So, here it is. I need another Renoir ASAP. And, I do mean ASAP. It has to fool all experts or those who call themselves experts. It must be flawless for the time period, and I want no excuses or screw-ups this time. Don't make the Picasso mistake. I certainly hope you have the two Monet paintings ready. You've had more than enough time for them. Here it is. I expect completion of everything in one week. ONE. WEEK.

"I won't tolerate anything less than perfect. I'll have my personal assistant pick up the Renoir. The Monets will be picked up tomorrow. And, if they don't meet with my satisfaction, I'll first cut off your hands and then kill you in ways you've never even heard of.

"DO I MAKE MYSELF CLEAR?"

Breathing hard, he punched the end call button and stared into the darkness.

"Idiot."

His second phone call went to another man in Venice, Italy. "The blonde is on her way to Venice. Yeah, he trailed her and will send you her info. Find her; scare her; rough her up, and make her paranoid. As usual, don't let her see you. Make it count. Okay? We'll finish her off later." He hung up, satisfied that job would be carried out.

"Now for the twit." The last phone call he made went to voicemail. He hung up, swearing to himself. Then, taking a deep breath, he decided to leave a cryptic message and called again. Throwing the phone into his fireplace, his evil grin returned. "There. That ought to make her think. My plan has started."

Champagne fueled the madness in his brain as he stumbled inside.

Chapter 3

IN THE PACIFIC Heights area of San Francisco, she paced. First, she walked with a purpose throughout most of the first floor in her stately home. Nothing about this wonderful home she had inherited registered with her like it usually did. Not the cloud-soft carpet in the hallway, nor the chef's kitchen where she ate her dinner, not even the richness of the small but elegant foyer. She was amazed and appreciative when her friend, George, left her this wonderful home. Usually, it calmed her with its beauty. But, not right now.

She was perturbed, angry, and perplexed, and she didn't like any of it. Walking past the well-stocked wine cellar for the second time, she opened the door. "I have to get a grip. Calm down. Think, Suzie, think." Speaking to herself, she hastily grabbed the first bottle of wine she came to in the oversized, well-stocked cellar. She didn't even notice the vintage nor the wine until she uncorked it, poured a glass, and took a sip. "Wow. This is fantastic. What the hell did I open, anyway?"

Taking her glass and the bottle from the cellar to the comfort of the den, she turned on the fireplace, settled in on the overstuffed sofa, took another sip, closed her eyes, and tried to relax. Talking out loud helped her get her thoughts in order. "Okay. I need to think back to the beginning.

"First, the auction house had a small Picasso, a confirmed original. My clients, Mr. and Mrs. Ascot, wanted me to purchase it for them. They knew it was expensive, but they were okay with that." She took a sip of wine. "But, after I bid on it, some strange guy came up to me and accused me of taking his painting. I told him he was obviously mistaken, and he left." She ran her fingers through her long, chestnut colored hair as she recalled the chain of events.

"Then, since I was excited I had bought my first Picasso, I texted a picture of it to my friend, Marta. But, she thought something seemed off about one of the colors in it, and she wanted me to take another look at its provenance and then at the painting itself. Unfortunately, it had already been delivered to the Ascots. Damn. I shouldn't have been in such a hurry to get it to them, but we were all so excited.

"When I told Marta that, she called the auction house a couple of days later to ask questions. That's when they told her they had discovered some issues. They wanted the painting returned. Double Damn."

Suzie sat this way, deep in thought, for several minutes.

"Turns out, they had reason to believe it was a forgery. I still don't understand all of it, but they told me they were working on issues bigger than just that painting. Poor Mr. and Mrs. Ascot. They got thrown into the middle of this horrible mess. And, now they lost their money and their painting.

"Let's see, what did they tell me? Some courier, claiming to be sent from my shop, came to their house to pick up the painting, and they just gave it to him. I don't even have a courier.

"Okay, first thing tomorrow I need to visit with them. Their money and my reputation is on the line." She sighed, drank the last of her wine, took her glass and the bottle to the kitchen, and headed up the grand staircase to her bedroom suite.

"Okay, time for bed. Tomorrow has to be better."

Chapter 4

ENTERING HER SHOP in San Francisco the following morning, Suzie looked around at all the treasures. "I am a reputable art dealer, respected all over the world. I thought I was buying a genuine Picasso. Now, I find I was involved with a forgery." Gesturing as she talked to herself, she made her way to her office at the back, smiling and nodding to each painting, sculpture, and artifact in her showroom. They were her babies. She knew each one, where it came from, how old it was, and which of her clients should at least have an opportunity to view it, if not purchase it. That's why the Picasso confused her so much.

Entering her office, she noticed the red light blinking on her phone to indicate at least one voicemail. Most of her calls came through her cell phone, but some of her clients still preferred her office phone. Turning on the espresso machine, Suzie sat down and retrieved the voicemails. The first one came from the Ascots, who had paid a great deal for the Picasso mess . . . the same mess that had kept her tossing and turning last night.

"Hi, Suzie. It's Eileen Ascot. Tom and I have been talking and we are so glad you know what you're doing. We would have been so embarrassed if we hung that Picasso and then someone told us it was a forgery. We want you know it's not your fault and we wondered if you could come to the house sometime today? We want to talk to you about replacing it, and we just can't make it in to The City today. Parking is so terrible, and we'd rather talk here. Any time after one o'clock is good. Just let us know. Thanks so much."

Suzie glanced at her calendar and decided that would work today. She called to confirm, made a cappuccino, and retrieved the second voicemail. It was a hang-up with no message. The third one was spoken in a muffled, almost slurred, voice and made her lean in to hear the message better.

"I've got a painting my uncle willed to me. He always said it was valuable. I need the money and wondered if you want to buy it. I'll call later." The message ended.

"That wasn't the strangest message I've had, but it was close. Wonder if I can figure out what number it came from." Suzie looked at the readout on the phone, but it said private. Hitting the redial button was no help, either. She just heard a busy signal.

"I guess he'll have to call me back. I'm not going to worry about it. Probably nothing to it anyway." Her cell phone chirped. Looking at the screen, she noticed it was the animal rescue facility. Sipping her cup of coffee, she took notes, and told them today at four o'clock would work perfectly.

"I shouldn't get excited, but I can't help it. I may end up with a little companion today. Now, though, I need to get to work. I have to get out my notes from the Ascot's visit and think about what they like and what they might want."

$\mathcal{C}$hapter 5

HAVING ARRIVED BACK in Venice from Milan, Marta unpacked, talked to Shadow, and left to visit a small, but prestigious art gallery and shop. Tourists and vendors wandered by the front door, along one of the many canals. Having been here for a couple of hours, her notebook was full of observations, questions, and ideas.

As a travel consultant based in San Francisco, Marta took small groups of people throughout Italy. Some wanted cooking lessons, and she brought them to life-long cooks in Tuscany, where they learned to make pasta. Others wanted Prosecco tours, so she took them to her vineyards north of Venice, close to Valdobbiadene. Still others had been asking for art and museum tours lately. Many of these wanted to purchase quality artwork to add to their collections at home.

That's why she was spending this month learning exactly what each gallery, shop, and museum had to offer her clients, first in Milan and now in Venice.

Living in San Francisco most of the time, Marta still knew much about Italian art and was familiar with the history of Venice, partly due to her grandmother growing up here. In fact, her grandmother's family was part of a royal family a couple hundred years ago. Marta had the tiara, jewels, and special coins to prove it. Right now, those were on loan to the Ca' Rezzonico.

Having finished at this gallery, Marta closed her notebook and decided she needed to head to the Rialto Market for lunch and dinner supplies. But, she stopped as a man caught her eye. He seemed to be doing something to one of the paintings in the next room. That by itself wasn't odd. What caused her to sit still and watch him was the painting he was removing . . . and then seemingly re-hanging.

From where she sat, she didn't think he could see her, but she lowered her head slightly, her blonde hair sweeping forward to block her face from his view. He had already removed a fairly small painting off the wall and placed it in a non-descript, brown box on the floor. Marta thought to herself that was a poor choice of boxes to hold a painting. Next, he took a painting he had sitting by the bench and hung it in its place. He wasn't in a hurry. His off-white gloves, dark blue cap, and gray jumpsuit were just as non-descript as the box by his feet. It was as if nothing was meant to be noticed. Or, remembered.

Marta watched as he closed the box, looked around, and exited through the back of that room. She could have sworn the painting he removed was exactly the same as the one he replaced. Looking around and seeing no one, she walked over to the wall where the workman had just been. She looked at her notebook, and discovered she had written notes about this exact painting. As she looked more closely, the hair on the back of her neck stood up. A chill raced up and down her spine as she looked around.

"Damn. Not again. This is just like in Milan two days ago. What the hell is going on? I need to talk to the owner and then call Clark." Wanting to see where that workman went, she walked into the next room toward the back wall where he exited. She saw no one and no obvious door. "Huh. I'm positive he went this way. Wonder where he is? This is getting more bizarre by the minute, and I don't like it."

She gathered her notebook, put everything in her large purse, and headed toward the front door, where two men stood quietly talking.

"Thank you for stopping." Dressed in shades of gray, from his perfectly knotted tie to his Italian leather loafers, one man smiled broadly and extended his smooth hand to Marta. "I hope you enjoyed our little gallery and shop. Please come back and visit again."

"I'm sure I will. I do have a question, though."

"Perhaps I will be able to answer your question."

"I thought I saw a workman in the far room. He appeared to be taking one painting off the wall and replacing it with the very same one. Then, he disappeared before I could ask him about the painting. Do you know what he was doing?"

Marta noticed the smile disappeared for a brief instant. "No one has been in that back room except for you. I'm sure you are mistaken."

Marta nodded but continued. "I was curious about the painting he was working with and . . . " She didn't get to finish her sentence before being interrupted by the well-dressed man.

"Thank you again for stopping." His glowing smile was replaced by a steely grimace.

Marta tried once more. "I really would like to talk to him about the painting."

Glancing briefly at Marta, he curtly nodded his head as he turned toward the bulky man standing beside him, in essence dismissing Marta.

"Thank you." Marta nodded to his back, smiled at the other man, and exited into the street. No one returned her smile.

Marta thought about the brief, stilted conversation and shook her head in confusion. "Okay. Not good. What didn't Mr. Too Perfect like about my questions? Does he know what that guy was doing? For that matter, what was he doing?" She frowned as she reflected on both men.

"They were an interesting pair by the door. No one looks that perfect. Not a hair out of place, immaculately creased trousers, and color coordinated to the max. And, his beefy friend is probably a guard, now that I think about it. But, a well-dressed guard. I'm positive their stylish shoes alone cost more than many people pay for rent. I know the guard was armed and his muscles strained in his tailored suit. Even I could see that. Time to call Clark as soon as I get home."

She headed toward the market.

Chapter 6

WHEN MARTA'S PHONE rang, she pulled it from her bag, looked at the screen, smiled, and answered it. "Clark, I'm so glad you called. I was just thinking about you."

"Funny thing, I was thinking about you and hoped you made it back safely to Venice. Anything more on the man by the train?"

"No. I just don't know. Maybe my imagination was working overtime."

"I highly doubt you imagined anything. You have a good eye for detail, and I'm glad you're paying attention to your surroundings. Now, the real reason I called is to see if you can spare a few days in Paris on your way back to San Francisco. I'd love to show you my latest favorite spots and talk to you about some paintings I'm working on. But, mainly I'd really like to spend some time with you, non-work time. Maybe we can actually talk about us. I'd like to get to know the real Marta better and see about taking this to the next level. What do you think?"

Marta smiled at the phone. She was hoping to get to know Clark better, but didn't want to get in the way of his crazy schedule. "Clark, I would love that."

"Great. What's your schedule like?"

"I don't have another group coming for a month. I purposely set it up that way so I could get back to San Francisco before the next tour came. I was planning on leaving here in a couple of days. You remember Suzie, our friend who turned her inheritance into a successful art consulting and sales business? She's had a couple of issues and would like some help, so I told her I could help better from there instead of from here. Shadow and I will be using Mario's jet to get back home. I am so spoiled with that plane. Shadow gets to go back and forth with me, and it's such a terrific way to fly. What would I do without Mario?"

"Yeah, Mario's plane is the only way to go! It's fantastic you and he could connect and become such great friends, especially after his grandfather and your grandmother were best friends. And, since Mario and his wife don't use the plane that much, it's generous of him to let you use it. Do you think he would mind if you and Shadow stopped here in Paris for a couple of days on your way home?"

"I'll talk to Mario and his pilot and get back to you. Shadow and I could be ready to leave as early as tomorrow or the next day."

"Fantastic. Be sure to tell your crazy cat I can't wait to see him, too. You can both stay with me in my apartment. I'll get some food for him and a bed. By the way, what's he think of flying? You don't have to drug him, do you?"

"No drugs. He's never thrilled with getting to the airport, because he has to be in his carrier. He yowls the whole way to the plane. Once on board though, he settles down on his bed, takes a bath, and then sleeps. Since his papers and vaccinations are in order, we have a special license to take him on board a private plane. The flight attendant loves him."

"I can imagine. He's a big sweetie. Make your calls and let me know when to pick you up. Okay?"

"Sure thing. But, I need to talk to you about a strange encounter here at an art gallery."

"I don't like the sound of that, especially after what just happened in Milan. What's going on?"

"It's a long story, but I had the same gut feeling I did in Milan about that Renoir forgery."

"What's up? Your gut is usually right on. Do you want to talk now?"

"First I'll call Mario and then get back to you in an hour. I can put my thoughts in order. Okay?"

"I'll be here. Stay safe."

Chapter 7

AFTER MAKING HER phone call to Mario and buying lunch supplies, Marta headed towards her villa, still thinking about the workman and the painting.

When her grandmother died, she left her small Venetian villa to Marta, which was a peaceful home during her stays in Venice. Marta had put special touches on her Italian home, mixing her grandmother's flair in with hers. Converting one of the three bedrooms into an office gave her a perfect place to work when she was in Italy. Photos of the vineyard she co-owned in the hills of the Veneto covered her walls of the office. Throughout the rest of the villa, she had placed photos of her travels and a few small paintings. Shadow, her big, fluffy, Maine Coon cat loved sitting in the third floor windows watching birds and people, and napping in the sun.

Checking the time, she decided she had just enough to visit one more gallery and shop on the way home. Since it featured local and regional Italian artists, she thought this would be a good shop to add to her tour. She walked as she talked to herself, creating her to-do list out loud. "Then, I need to get home and write down my thoughts about that painting. I really can't wait to see Clark. And, I can't wait to find out more about his comment that we should get to know each other better. Wonder what he meant by the next level. I guess Shadow and I will find out in a couple of days."

She stopped in front of the shop's highly polished glass doors. Just as she reached for the oversized, twisted, gold handle, the door flew open, and a man charged out of the shop. Had she not been quick on her feet, she'd be sprawled on the cobblestone sidewalk with her groceries and lunch supplies scattered all over. "Whoa. Watch where you're going." She barely had time to jump out of his way, as she dropped her bags to the sidewalk, and ended up against the building.

Glaring at his retreating back, she was ready to yell at him when something stopped her. "Why does he remind me of the guy at the last museum? His grey jumpsuit and blue cap look almost the same. But, then again, that's probably a standard uniform for workers. I need to check inside to see what they can tell me."

Regaining her composure and picking up her bags, Marta entered the softly lit, quiet shop and gallery. Immediately, she was greeted by a stunning woman, whose tailored-to-fit suit of deep plum hugged her every curve. Impossibly high heels, exactly the color of the suit, completed her runway-looking ensemble. Marta couldn't help but think to herself that next to this woman, she was horribly underdressed, even in the middle of the day. Her black pants, silk, crimson shirt, and black, cashmere sweater paled in comparison on every level. This woman could have just stepped out of a glossy, modeling magazine. Self-consciously Marta straightened up and tried to look a little bit professional after her recent encounter outside the front door.

"Welcome. If you would like specific information about an artist or sculptor, I would be happy to assist you. If you have any questions, I can answer those as well. Otherwise, please take your time and enjoy." With a perfect smile showing just the right amount of perfect white teeth behind lipstick that matched her suit, she gestured to the pieces on display near the front and went to stand behind her desk.

"Thank you, Simone." Marta looked at her name tag as she spoke. "Did you just have a workman come rushing out of here?" She pointed to the front door.

"Not that I know of. Did you need some work done on something?"

"No." Marta shook her head. "It's just that he about ran over me as I was entering. He seemed familiar, and I wondered if it was the same man I just saw at another gallery."

"I'm sorry about that. But, no one left here recently." Simone almost smiled and shrugged her shoulders, then went back to looking at something on her desk.

Confused and perplexed, Marta thanked Simone and made a quick tour of the small gallery. As she left, she gave Simone a business card and told her she would be in touch with her as a possible stop for her tours. Simone took her card. "Thank you. That would be something you need to visit with the owner about, however. He's not here right now."

"I understand, Simone. Do you have his card or how is it best to get in touch with him?"

"His name is Sir Antonio Furst, and he's in London right now. I will tell him you were here and give him your information."

"Thank you. Is there a way I can contact him directly?"

"No. I'm sorry. He doesn't take calls. He'll call you." With each exchange Simone became a little more distant, her eyes narrowing.

Marta thanked her again and left. Once outside she thought of another question and returned to the gallery, expecting to ask Simone. No one was around. Simone had disappeared; the lights had dimmed, and the quiet echoed. "Hello. Simone? Are you in the back?"

Nothing. "That's strange. In fact, this is the oddest experience. Maybe she had to use the restroom.

"Simone. Are you still here?" Again, nothing. Marta started toward the next room, but the lights had gone completely dim, and all she could see were shadows. Glancing around, Marta decided she had better things to do than track down a gallery employee that didn't want her business. "Guess I won't put this one on the next tour. It doesn't meet my criteria after all."

Leaving the shop for the second time, Marta had only walked a few feet when she felt someone brush up against her. Since there weren't a lot of people on the narrow sidewalk, she automatically moved over. "Scusami." Before she could turn to look at the person, she was body-slammed into the wall, causing her to stumble.

With a vise-like grip crushing her arm, his knee pressing into her back, and his other arm ramming her face into the stone wall, he hissed his warning at the back of her head. "Leave it alone. You didn't see nothin'. Keep askin' questions, and you'll be sorry. One more move and you're dead." Her five-foot, two-inch slightly built frame was no match for the bulky, muscular, tall attacker.

Since her face was up close and personal with the wall, she couldn't take a breath, let alone scream. Glancing down, all she could see were his feet, clad in black running shoes. Squirming slightly, Marta tried to twist away from him. That caused him to tighten the grip on her arm, creating numbing, shooting pains. Just as she was thinking of how she could get positioned to kick him, he increased the pressure on her back, forcing his knee into her spine. Breathing and swallowing became difficult. With his arm, he forced her face harder against the wall, brutally scraping her cheek and forehead. Then, as abruptly as he grabbed her, he let go and disappeared. Marta took a deep breath and steadied herself against the wall. As soon as she regained her balance, she hurried to where he had gone. No one was there.

"What the hell was that about?" She rubbed her sore forehead and bruised cheek. Her fingers came away bloody.

Chapter 8

EARLIER, IN THE hills north of Venice, Serge awoke after a short night of restless sleep. Yawning and stretching, he spoke as the morning sun made its way into his small, but well-furnished, home nestled in those dark green hills. "Damn. Why was I dreaming someone was chasing me, trying to kill me? I hate that. The last time I had that very same dream, I was beat up. I don't need that again."

Shaking his head to clear out the disturbing dream, he walked next door to his art studio to survey his latest works. He smiled. "Good. Damn good, if I do say so myself. These look exactly like the original Monet paintings. In fact, I'm getting better by the day. I do believe it's time I asked for more money. What he's been paying me is peanuts, and he's getting high quality pieces. Not a fair trade. Not a fair trade at all."

Moving each one to his table, he continued. "I'm glad I decided to tell him I'm finished. Too many things have been bothering me lately, and I'm really beginning to wonder what he does with these. It can't be good, and I don't want to be a part of it. I'm glad I've been taking some precautions. Not sure if anything will come of it, but it never hurts to be prepared."

Taking his time, Serge carefully wrapped each painting in plain brown paper, stacked them in a crate, added some of his special, extra paper for packing, and set them by the door. "There. They are ready for the courier to pick them up today." Moving his bottle of wine out of the way, he noticed it was empty. "Damn. That bottle didn't last long. Guess I'll have coffee first and then head to the village to get some more wine."

His phone made a slight chirp, and he looked at it. "Huh. He called again. He's probably anxious about these three paintings. I have half a mind to withhold them until he pays me more. Maybe I will. He can afford it." He gestured as he spoke toward his phone.

Then, listening to the voicemail, he almost dropped the phone when he heard the last part. "What the hell. What does he mean, screw up? I didn't screw anything up. I painted exactly what he asked.

"I think he's losing it. He makes less sense every time he calls. Okay. It's past time to end this arrangement. These threats just confirmed that for me. I'm going to send him a text to his special number as soon as I get back from town. In the meantime, I'll just hang on to these sweet little Monets, and I'll only start on his rush job after he pays me what I'm worth. Then, good riddance to him."

Feeling better after his self-pep talk, Serge gathered his jacket and headed into the village. His first stop was the bar, where he met his good friend Harry. After he filled Harry in on his plans and had a couple of espressos, he had him listen to the voicemail. Harry cautioned him. "Man, I don't like the sounds of that. Are you sure you want to work for a guy like that? You could make tons more money painting legit stuff for people. I have plenty of contacts who would pay big bucks. And, you wouldn't have to put up with that crap. I think you need to be careful of him. That voicemail is creepy and sounds like a threat to me."

"Harry, you read my mind. I'm asking for more money for the ones I already have finished. I'll do his rush job, and then I'm done. He can find some other poor chap to badger."

Harry nodded, "Good plan, man. In fact, I'd say the sooner the better. By the way, I'll be out to your house tomorrow to work more on your garden. It will be finished in two weeks or less."

Serge thanked him, nodded goodbye, left the bar, and headed to the wine shop where he purchased a case of wine. "Might as well celebrate my new plan. Soon I'll be able to afford the really good stuff. I'm glad Harry suggested doing my own painting. I'm tired of copying other people, anyway."

Chapter 9

TWO DAYS LATER, Marta and Shadow were reunited with Clark after an uneventful flight to Paris. "It's so good to see you both, and I'm glad you are able to spend a few days with me here in one of my favorite cities." Clark kissed Marta and gave Shadow a rub on his head as he let him out of his carrier. Shadow purred briefly and went about inspecting the entire apartment. "Will he be okay here while we head out to lunch and then to my office?"

"Absolutely. He's adaptable and will probably be asleep in the sun before we know it. He doesn't mind traveling but isn't wild about the carrier. Let's go. I'm starved, and I can't wait to see what you're working on."

Clark looked closely at Marta as he gently touched her cheek. "What's this scrape on your cheek? It looks nasty."

"I'll explain later."

They walked to a café where they talked during a lunch of rich cheesy quiche, perfectly dressed green salad, warm flaky croissants, and a carafe of rose wine. Taking Marta's hand, Clark looked at her. "I hope we're both on the same wavelength here. I meant what I said about getting to know you better. In fact, maybe we can spend more time together once this case is finished, take some time off, and forget about work for a little while. Would that work?"

Marta smiled. "Absolutely. Let's get this case and my next trip out of the way and then go somewhere special." They talked about favorite cities, places they both had been, and places they wanted to visit. "I'm excited. I could start looking at airfare and accommodations for a month from now, or is that too soon?"

"That works for me. Surprise me."

"Fantastic." Marta's head was already in travel planning mode, but she switched gears and inquired about the paintings Clark had been investigating.

"Long, messy story. This started out as a couple of simple consulting jobs. Two different art collectors wanted a third party to look at their pieces. The first one bought a small painting at an auction in the south of France. He was pleased with it, regardless of whether it was worth anything or not. He brought it home, had the painting and the provenance authenticated, and discovered he had a valuable piece of art. Quite valuable. Needless to say, he was ecstatic. Since the frame was pretty damaged, he took it to a reputable, or so he thought, frame shop to have the frame repaired.

"The process took a whole lot longer than he was originally told, even with him checking on it weekly. When he finally received his painting and repaired frame back, he hung it up and didn't think a lot about it. He liked what they had done with the frame, and he was happy once again.

"Fast forward about two months to when a friend was looking at it closely. The friend remarked that it was too bad one of the corners of the painting had been severely damaged and inquired whether it was always that way or if the framer had done it. James, the owner, took it off the wall, and they both inspected it much more closely. James had not remembered seeing that corner so beat up and told his friend he was sure he would have noticed that. Since he had taken some photos of it, he compared those to the painting. What he discovered was, that corner was not damaged in his photos. It was obvious, really obvious.

"The next day, he went to the frame shop. Guess what? It was no longer there. So, now he's having ugly thoughts, wondering if the shop was in trouble for not handling paintings correctly. Another friend suggested he call me to take a look at the painting and try to figure out how the corner was damaged."

"It's weird the shop would be gone. What did you find out?"

"First, I looked at the painting, and several things bothered me. The material wasn't quite right; the paint looked too good, things like that. Then, I went to where the shop was and asked other business owners nearby what they knew about it. Their answers were all about the same, and not good. One even told me he thought the shop was a front for some illegal business, as the people that came all hours of the day and night were, in his opinion, thugs."

"What?"

"I know. So, my next stop was the police. Apparently, that shop was under suspicion as a front for stolen paintings. That led me to Interpol and my friend, Ian. They had just become involved when the shop disappeared."

"Disappeared? A shop can't just disappear, can it?"

"You wouldn't think so, but this one did. Which makes Interpol suspicious of who was running it. They had to have quite the organization behind them to vanish overnight. In fact, Interpol had just placed two men across the street as waiters in a café, and they were working with the owner of the café the first night. The frame shop was dark, nothing unusual going on. They left the café about 11 that night and two more agents were going to be watching the shop from above the café. Those agents were delayed as their car had two flat tires. Two."

"Uh oh."

"Yep. You can probably guess the rest. By the time they had the tires changed and got to the street, the frame shop had paper covering the window. Of course, they went around back. The back door was ajar, and when they entered, they found nothing. Nothing. Not even a scrap of paper.

"It was quick, efficient, and completely a professional job, according to the agents. Ian called me to let me know."

"What did you do?" Marta took another bite as she watched Clark. She knew he was deciding what he could tell her.

Chapter 10

"I WENT BACK to James and looked at his painting some more. I have some opinions, but I would also like yours. I've got it at the office."

"I hope I can help. I'm not nearly as proficient at looking for issues like you are, though."

"Maybe not, but you always see things from a different perspective and that's what I need."

"Okay. But, you said there were two collectors. What's the deal with the other one?"

"That gentleman bought a painting from the same auction facility but at a different time. These weren't exclusive auctions, mind you. In the world of collecting art, auctions and sales like these happen periodically, and there are quite a few auction sites or houses that are small-time. Needless to say, they're not all ultra-famous, either. There can be paintings or different works from newer or undiscovered artists who need to start somewhere small, or things from estate sales that have been in someone's home or attic for decades. Still, some of these paintings and pieces can go for several hundred thousand Euros. So, it's not small peanuts.

"Anyway, he bought a piece by a relatively new artist and had it hanging in his office waiting room for a couple of months. His name is George, and he's an attorney with an office in a prominent area here in Paris. One day, a new client came to him. That client proceeded to ask him where he got the painting hanging in the waiting room. George told him his story, and then asked if he'd heard of this new artist.

"Turns out, his new client is the artist. Only problem is, something is wrong with the painting."

"What do you mean?"

"Apparently, according to the artist, he noticed something missing in the painting. He always paints something in his work, known pretty much only to him and those who study his work. That symbol was missing. He told George he thinks someone copied his painting."

"Did he have this painting in the auction, though?"

"That's another curious piece of the puzzle. He did not. Originally it was listed, but a private buyer contacted the auction company and bought it. So, it wasn't listed nor was it in the final auction."

"But how was George able to bid on it and purchase it if it wasn't there? I'm confused."

"So was George. He and the artist contacted the auction company and guess what? They don't answer their phone. Since I don't believe in coincidences, I called Ian again. Interpol did not have them on their radar but they do now. As of now, it's an open investigation. We're working together to figure out what happened."

"What about the artist? Didn't you say someone else bought his original painting prior to the auction?"

"Yes, and we've finally traced who that is. His name was buried in corporations, shell corporations, and all sorts of complicated webs. For some reason, he seems to be a recluse or at least doesn't want his name out there. It's still confusing."

"So, what's his name, and what does he do?"

"We're not sure what he does. He lives in several places, mostly London, according to what we found out. His name is Sir Antonio Furst."

Chapter 11

MARTA CHOKED ON her sip of wine. "Whoa. I know you don't believe in coincidences, but I just heard that name a couple days ago."

"Marta, what do you mean? Do you know him? Is he in Venice?"

"Okay, let me fill you in on Venice and the things bothering me there. First, the text I sent you about the train. I know I was being followed, and even saw the same guy several times. Then, there's an issue with a painting." Marta explained the bizarre incident with the workman. Clark nodded with a puzzled look, and Marta continued. "I had notes about the first painting he took off the wall for my brochure, and I know he hung up the exact same one. Only, the second one is a forgery. I'm almost positive. It's glaringly clear. Just like Milan. I'd bet a lot of money on it.

"Anyway, when he was finished, he disappeared in the back of the gallery. I looked for him after he left, and couldn't even find a door. Nothing. It was like he disappeared into thin air. To top that off, the owner or manager said no one was there except me. And, that's not true. When I tried to talk to him, he became uninterested in continuing the conversation and literally dismissed me."

She related her visit to the second shop. "I'm positive the woman at the front told me the owner's name was Antonio Furst. I don't remember if she said Sir in front of his name, but how many men have that name? That whole visit was odd, anyway."

"No, you're right about the name. But, what do you mean the visit was odd?"

"First, like I said, I was almost knocked down, and I swear it was the same workman as I saw in the first shop. Yet, the lady at the front desk dismissed my questions and even told me no one had been there. Again, not true. Then, after I left, I thought of another question and went back in. The lights were so dim it was like they were in the process of turning off, and no one was around. Not even the lady at the front desk. So, I left. But, it was kind of a creepy feeling. And, the lady was scary in a don't-mess-with-me way."

"Hmm. I'm going to let Ian know about both of those shops. We may have a strong connection to Milan."

"Clark, there's one more thing. It has to do with this scrape on my cheek." Marta explained about the man who grabbed her and the warning he hissed at her.

"Marta, I don't like that at all. Are you okay? Did you get any description of the guy?"

"Not much. He grabbed me from behind, and from what I could tell he had on all black. I'd guess he was at least as tall as you, maybe taller. So, around six-foot-three or so. He seemed to be bulkier than you, but that could be what he was wearing. That's it."

"Ian needs to know about this as well. Any idea what he meant when he told you to stop asking questions?"

"None. I had just come from both shops where I asked about the workman. But, that wasn't really anything threatening. I've been trying to think, and I can't come up with anything I've asked questions about lately. I don't get it. Maybe he had the wrong person."

"I doubt it. I would bet it has to do with the painting you saw. You need to be careful." Clark looked directly at her when he said it. "I mean it. I don't want to lose you."

"I will. Now tell me about the second painting. The one George bought. What did he and the artist do?"

"The artist apologized to George and is painting one for him. We have the one which the artist says is a fake. The artist also gave us another to use for comparison. I want you to look at both of these as well. You may see something we have missed."

"I don't really understand what is going on. Why have originals and fakes? If, indeed, they really are fakes?"

"That's the part we're working on right now. Who benefits? Why do they benefit? Why go to all the trouble of creating a forgery for a painting that also exists? Who's doing the forgeries? Does this Sir Antonio Furst fit into more of the puzzle than just the one painting? Does the frame shop fit into this mix, and . . ." Clark's cell phone chirped. "Excuse me, Marta. I need to take this call from Ian."

Marta sipped the last of her wine while Clark walked to the sidewalk to talk to Ian. Shaking his head, he returned and sat down. "One more piece of the puzzle. The auction site I mentioned? It's gone, closed up, the building totally stripped, nothing left. And, there's more."

"You're kidding? When was the last time anyone was there? What do you mean, there's more?"

"Some of Ian's guys had talked to the owner a week ago. Everything looked good, including the facility, their records, their finances, the whole works. This morning one of the agents received a call from another shop owner in the area, telling him he saw many moving vans there about midnight the last two nights. At first, he thought more things were coming for another auction. Apparently, moving vans drop off items quite often. But, when he saw them the second night at midnight, they seemed to be loading things into the van. He became suspicious.

"So, this morning he walked over there. From the front, everything looked okay. When he walked around to the back of the larger warehouse, he noticed something that caused him to call the agent. He thought he saw blood seeping out from under the back door."

"Blood? What happened?"

"The agent told him to go home, and they would be there to investigate. When the agents arrived, they found a body inside the warehouse that served as storage for the auction house. It was the owner of the facility. He had been tortured and shot."

"Oh dear. What's going on, Clark? Is all of this connected? Didn't you mention some other galleries who thought they had forgeries?"

"Yeah. There are two small galleries here in Paris. Something isn't right with them, either. Both places had purchased paintings. Everything was legit up to the point where a contractor came to do some work in the galleries. In one incident the gallery initiated the work, and in the second one there was a water leak that needed to be fixed. After the contractors left, both gallery owners discovered a couple of their paintings had been replaced with forgeries. Or, at least those were their suspicions. I've checked them out, and they are right. Forgeries. Good ones, however. It's puzzling, but it appears someone wants original paintings and doesn't want to pay for them.

"Ian seems to think all of this is connected; the forgeries, the thefts, the murders. We just need a common denominator. Now, let's go to my office." Clark took Marta's face in his hands and looked at her scrapes more closely.

"I'm still concerned about you being attacked. I have this feeling you're part of it. And, that bothers me. A lot."

Chapter 12

AS MARTA TOOK time looking at the two paintings in Clark's office workroom and making some notes, Clark met with Ian and some other men from Interpol in a conference room. When they were finished, Ian greeted Marta. "Good to see you again. Hopefully, this is more pleasant than our Milan visit, although Clark told me about what just happened in Venice, and I'm going to send an agent to check things out. We need to keep an eye on you. Wouldn't want you to get involved in any more espionage dealings with certifiably unbalanced criminals."

"Thanks, Ian. I hope I'm done with those types. And, I have no idea what that guy who attacked me in Venice was talking about. I've racked my brain, and nothing comes to mind."

"I don't need to impress upon you to stay alert. But, do be careful. Now, I'll let you and Clark get to work on these, and then we can add your comments to our files. How long are you here?"

"Just for a few days. I need to finish my tour planning for the next group and visit with a friend in San Francisco. She bought what was supposed to be a genuine small Picasso, but there are issues with it. It may be a forgery. They want it back, but it's gone. It seems like it's a mess for her. I'm headed there next."

"That wouldn't be Suzie, would it?"

"Yeah, Ian, it is. Why?"

"She left me a voicemail just this morning, and I think she said she left one for you as well. She mentioned that Picasso painting, and the fact that it seems to have been stolen from her clients. Then, on top of that, she received two calls from a man who says he has a valuable painting his uncle left to him, and he's bringing it to her. He says it's a Renoir. I believe she just wants some direction on how to proceed. I told her I would get back to her."

As Ian was talking, both Marta and Clark checked their phones, and both had voicemails from Suzie.

"Ian, how do you want to proceed on this?"

"Let's call Suzie right now and give her some direction. Do you remember Pete, our undercover agent who worked with us in London? He's in San Francisco right now. I'll call him, too, as I want him to be with Suzie when she meets with the caller. We need an agent on this, and he'll be able to tell us what's going on."

Ian, Marta, and Clark placed a conference call to Suzie and to Pete to go over the plan Ian developed on short notice. "Suzie and Pete, I'm introducing you on this conference call. Pete, you can go to Suzie's shop and meet face to face.

"Suzie, in light of some issues with similar artwork here in France, we want to proceed carefully on this one. This guy could have just an old copy of a Renoir painting that hung in his uncle's garage, or he could be trying to unload something he thinks is valuable, or we could have something worth paying attention to. But, whatever it is, we don't want to alert him that anything is wrong or we're suspicious of anything. I think Pete should be there to view the painting when he brings it in. Does that make sense?"

"Yes, but how do I explain Pete?"

"You can introduce Pete as one of your most trusted clients who has an eclectic collection of art and is always looking for good pieces to add. You can say you thought of him as a buyer for this painting. In fact, you could mention Pete has more available cash to spend on art than you do right now.

"Pete, I want you to observe everything about the man, the deal, etc. You know the drill. Suzie, you should be your professional self. Do exactly what you would do if anyone brought a piece for you to look at. Be pleasant and try to get him to relax.

I bet he won't be there long anyway. Did he give any idea of how much he wants for the painting?"

"Not really. He said his uncle always told him it was worth a lot of money. I tried to ask where his uncle lived and how long he had the painting, but he said he had to go and hung up. How do you want me to proceed with questioning him, examining the painting, and offering him money? Normally, with something of this caliber, I would give a small down payment in good faith and then have it more closely and professionally inspected."

"I understand. Do a cursory review of it, enough for you to get a gut feeling if it's real or not. I know that will be tough, though."

"Pete is an art expert as well. Pete, I don't want you to inspect the painting like you would for forgeries. Make the guy think his painting impresses you. Tell him it would look great in your grand foyer or wherever the hell makes sense. You know what you're doing."

"Ian, will do. I should be able to form a quick assessment. Of course, we won't know for certain if it's the original that was stolen or if it's a good fake. Like Suzie says, that's going to take some time. We need to have him leave it here."

"Understood. But, we also have to assume he's not going to want to do that. Both of you will have to think quick if it comes to him wanting to run. This may just turn out to be a Renoir that was recently stolen, and if that's the case, we don't want to lose this trail."

"Ian, what if I can get him to leave it for just the day? Maybe give him a good faith down payment?"

"Suzie, that would be ideal. If you can, go for it. Then, you and Pete can look it a little more thoroughly and take quality photos. But, you'll have to give him some money. Pete, do you have that taken care of?"

"Yes. I can write a check, which he probably won't take. For back up, I have $25,000 in marked bills. That should work as a down payment until we nab him."

"Okay, Suzie and Pete. Good luck, and let us know how it goes." They disconnected the call.

$\mathscr{C}$hapter 13

"PETE'S A GOOD guy to be with Suzie, but they don't have much to go on. My gut tells me the guy won't even show up."

"True, Ian. But, then again, maybe he somehow acquired this stolen painting and needs the money."

"Guys, would someone go to this trouble if the painting was a fake? If it's a good fake, wouldn't you think the black market would be a better place to sell it? A high end, reputable shop in a major city seems kind of the wrong place to unload a fake. To me, at least."

"Marta, you're probably right. If the guy shows, he may need to unload it quickly. He might have stolen it from the original thief and needs to be rid of it. We'll just have to wait and see. Did they say he was supposed to be there in the next couple of days?"

"I think so."

"Switching gears, Marta, did you notice anything on the paintings Clark has here?"

"I almost forgot, Ian. I made some notes and have some questions."

"Good. Let's go look at those now."

The three walked into Clark's back office, and Marta explained what she saw and the questions she had. When she was finished, Clark looked at Ian. "This is why I wanted her to look at these. I've looked at them so many times; I was hoping I wasn't just trying to see things that weren't there. Great eye for detail, Marta."

"Thanks. These are just my thoughts, and I don't have anything to go on. The first one could be an original, or it could be a fake. It's good; I'll give it that. Since I know how you work, I imagine you are making sure the paint is from the right period of time and all of that. To me, it just has a fresh look to it. Nothing I can put my finger on. It just looks good. Maybe too good for having been around all this time. The brush strokes are how they should be; the backing material looks right, but it bothers me. That's about all I can say about that one."

"I completely agree, Marta. And, yes you are correct. The paint is being authenticated as we speak. I probably won't get the results back for another week or so. The backing bothers me, too. It's a little too stiff for my take, considering the year. We'll see what the lab says about it as well. What about the second one?"

"Well, that one was fun. This new artist must have a sense of humor to go along with his talent. And, I would not have noticed anything off if I hadn't been looking for something out of the ordinary. Nothing in any research tells what he does. No one is going to know about this unless you've talked to him or are seriously looking for something.

"He has a great eye for color, and his landscapes are watery, but not so that you don't recognize them. I like what he does. They're mellow somehow. And, I found his symbol. He places a small gray kitten in every painting. It's not obvious, it could pass for a couple of brush strokes, and I bet a lot of viewers don't even see it. The kitten is in a different pose and seems to blend right into the landscape. But, he's there in every one. It's great.

"That kitten is missing in the painting your client purchased, Clark. It's nowhere to be seen. I triple-checked. That one is most definitely a copy or a fake or whatever you want to call it."

"Right again. The artist was most upset at someone copying his work and wants us to find out what is going on." Clark turned to Ian.

"I need to work some more with the gallery owners here as well as the artist. Is there anything else you need from either Marta or me in the meantime?"

"No. I'm heading south to help with the investigation of the murdered auction house owner. There are some things about it we haven't told anyone, and I want to get to work on that one as soon as possible. I'll leave these forgeries to you, Clark, and hopefully you can work on them ASAP. And, let's all stay in touch with Suzie and Pete in San Francisco. Marta, stay safe. When do you head there?"

"I'm leaving in two days and don't come back to Venice for a couple of weeks."

Clark hugged Marta as he kissed her. "So much for spending time together. We'll postpone our getaway for a little while. Okay?"

Marta nodded, silently wondering when that would be.

*C*hapter 14

IN SAN FRANCISCO, Suzie finished her conference
call with Ian, Clark, Marta, and Pete and turned to the overstuffed
pet bed in the corner. "Lady, I hope you're adjusting to the shop.
It's just about time for our walk." The part Siberian Husky, part
German Shepard, looked up and thumped her tail. "Perhaps you
understand the word walk." At the second mention of walk, her tail
thumped harder.

"I'm glad the rescue place showed you to me. Originally, I
thought I wanted a cute, little lap dog, but you have certainly won
my heart in just one day. I'm so glad they let me take you. I know
they'll send me the rest of the information on you. You are so special. And, you're beyond smart. Let's take our walk now, and I can
get some coffee."

Suzie and Lady left the shop, locked the door behind them,
and stepped onto the sidewalk. When the light turned green and
the walk sign lit up, Suzie glanced both ways, and stepped off the
curb into the street. Lady jerked hard on her leash to pull Suzie
back to the sidewalk as a dark colored sedan came flying through
the intersection. As Suzie tripped on the curb and lay sprawled on
the sidewalk, two pedestrians came to her side.

"Miss, if that dog of yours hadn't pulled you out of the way, you'd be dead." A well-dressed man knelt down to see if Suzie was hurt. "Are you okay?"

"I think so. My knee hurts, but I don't see any blood. Did you see what happened?"

"You had the walk light, and I was only a few feet behind you, going to cross the street. But this car came out of nowhere, speeding up as he hit the intersection. Now that I think about it, he swerved right at you. Must have been drunk or high." He shook his head. "I just called the police."

By now, a few more people had gathered and confirmed what the first man was saying. "Yeah. He came at you, alright. Your dog is a hero."

"Thanks, everyone. This is my new dog . . . and now my lifesaver." Suzie hugged Lady. As the bystanders helped Suzie to her feet, a police car pulled up. After the officer questioned any witnesses, he finished with questions for Suzie as they walked back to her shop. "You're sure you're okay?"

"I'm fine. But, I still need to take Lady for a walk. That's what we were going to do."

"I'll walk with you. We may need to ask you some more questions later. Okay?"

"Sure. No problem. Come on, Lady, let's get our walk in."

Once again, Lady wagged her tail at the mention of walk. As they headed to Washington Park, the officer said, "It's too bad no one got a better description of the car. Of course, if it was going as fast as everyone indicated, that's to be expected. Just be careful, and keep an eye out anytime you're near a crosswalk. Several witnesses said it seemed like the car veered toward you. That could be true, or it could be because the driver didn't have control, with as fast as they were going."

Suzie thanked him as they headed back to her shop. Rounding the corner, the officer noticed a man standing outside her entrance and put his hand on Suzie's arm. "Do you know him?"

"No. I don't."

"Stay back with your dog, and let me handle this, okay?"

Suzie hung back as the officer approached the tall man dressed in all black, from his jeans to his leather jacket to his boots. "Sir, may I help you?"

Looking at the policeman and then down the block at Suzie, he said something Suzie couldn't hear. Slowly reaching into an inside pocket he pulled out something Suzie couldn't quite see. She and Lady hung back until the officer motioned for them to come forward.

"Miss, this man says he has an appointment to talk with you. Is that correct?"

Just as Suzie was about to say she had never seen him before, he spoke up. "Suzie, I'm Pete Jensen. We talked on the phone about an hour ago."

"Ah, yes. Officer, I did speak to Pete, and he said he was coming by. In all the confusion, I completely forgot."

Chapter 15

INSIDE HER SHOP, the officer reminded Suzie to be careful and to call if she remembered anything else about the driver or the car.

"Suzie, what did he mean? And, what confusion? By the way, as an introduction, I'm Pete Jensen. And, who is this lovely animal?"

"Pete, nice to meet you. Lady, meet Pete. It's been quite the afternoon." Suzie filled him in on the events, shaking a little as she sat down. "Guess it's finally hitting me. Lady really saved my life. I just got her yesterday. And, now she's my hero."

Pete nodded as Suzie was talking, stroking Lady's head. "I don't like it. If those witnesses were right, and the driver was aiming for you, we need to keep an eye on you."

"I'm sure he was just trying to get through the light. It happens all the time. I'll be extra careful, but I don't think we need to worry."

Pete wasn't so sure, but kept his thoughts to himself. "Okay, Suzie, let's talk about the Renoir. I will be here before the guy gets here, and we can follow the basic plan Ian laid out. If anything gets funny or doesn't seem right to me, I'll tell you I have an appointment that I need to cancel. I'll make it sound like this painting is much more important to me than my appointment. Then, I'll make a call to cancel. I'll be sure to let him hear me do it so it doesn't seem like a set-up to him. In reality, I'll be calling another special agent, who will be close by. Sound okay, so far?"

"Okay. I'm not sure how much time I'll have to look at it. What if we buy it, and it's just a mediocre painting?"

"That's a chance we're willing to take. Let me fill you in on a little more of what I do and how I'm involved here."

"Great. Want a cup of coffee?"

"Better yet, are you finished here for the day?"

"Yes. Especially after the excitement. Why?"

"Let's go have a glass of wine, and I can give you the whole story. Is there somewhere Lady can go, too?"

"My friend owns a wine bar, and he lets well-mannered dogs inside. Let's go."

At the mention of go, Lady stood up and wagged her tail.

"This is one smart dog. Or, at least she likes to go."

Suzie's office phone rang, she answered it, listened for 15 seconds, and almost dropped it on the desk. Her hand trembled as she hung up and looked at Pete.

"Suzie, what the hell's wrong? You're white as a ghost, and you're shaking. Who was that?"

Grabbing Lady, Suzie buried her face in her fur, and then looked up at Pete. "It wasn't an accident."

"Okay. Start from the beginning. What did the caller want? What did he say?"

Taking a deep breath, Suzie looked at Pete. "As soon as I answered, a gruff, almost hoarse voice interrupted my normal greeting. These were his exact words. 'You were lucky. This time. Too bad.' Then he hung up."

Pete grabbed the phone and tried to reverse dial, but nothing came up. "Did you see what number he was calling from?"

"It said private."

"I can get a trace but it won't do us any good. The call was too short, and we're not sure if he's using that phone anymore anyway. I'm calling Officer Stone."

Chapter 16

WHILE PETE AND Officer Stone were talking, another phone conversation was taking place in San Francisco.

"Boss, I did exactly what you wanted. I grabbed a car and waited for her. I knew she would leave her shop sometime, and I was right. I sure did scare her. Yeah, I ditched the car. Wiped it clean, just like before. Then I left her the message. What? You want me to do that other part again? Sure, I can do that. It'll take a little time to get all the parts together. I know a guy here who sells the stuff I need. It will be like England and France. Right?

"But, how do I know where she'll be? Oh, I got it. Okay. Give me a couple of days or less. She won't expect a thing before the big boom." He started to say something else, but the call had already been disconnected.

"Huh. Guess he didn't want to hear my plan. Okay. Time to call Bruno and get started on building the thing. I'll show him I know what I'm doing. She won't be scared this time. She'll be a goner. This one is fool-proof."

Chapter 17

PETE FINISHED HIS phone conversation with Officer Stone and turned to Suzie. "The police want to put a tap on your phone in case you receive any more calls. Are you okay with that?"

"Sure. But, we don't want the police here when the guy comes to bring the painting, do we?"

"No, we don't. They're going to wait until they hear from either you or me. And, they will have some extra presence around. I told them about the meeting and to hold off on that as well. We don't need him recognizing police and staying away. I think that's all we can do for today. Let's go get that glass of wine, and I'll fill you in on a few things."

Pete, Suzie, and Lady left her shop and walked a couple of blocks to a small wine bar. Suzie greeted the owner as they entered. "Hey, Tom, is it okay if my new companions and I just sit in the back corner?"

"Hey, Suzie. How's it going? Is that a new dog? Sure, sit anywhere."

"Meet Lady, my new best friend. And, this is Pete, another friend."

Tom nodded to Pete and said hello to Lady, who sat politely as he gave her a quick pat on the head.

When they were settled, wine bottle in front of them, Pete began to fill Suzie in. "I've been an undercover Interpol agent for about six years. Before that, an instructor at Quantico. My dad was there. Kind of runs in the family. I'm one of those guys, like Clark, who can interact and get along with the FBI, Interpol, and with local police departments. I don't pose a threat to their egos or care about whose turf is more important.

"For the last several months I've been working closely with Ian on forgeries, especially in Italy and now in France. There are many small galleries or shops that have purchased originals, had them authenticated, have the provenance, and everything is good. Then, something happens. There's a water leak, and workmen come in, or there's a disturbance of some kind, and supposed undercover police come in. After all the commotion, the gallery or shop discovers they have a forgery. And, it's not the one that was originally hanging on their wall."

"Wait. I don't get it. I thought it was authenticated?"

"Right you are, Suzie. However, during whatever problem or disruption happened in the shop the paintings were switched. The workmen switched them or let someone in to do the switch. The forgeries were good enough so the owners didn't realize there had been a switch."

"I'm still confused. Why switch? And, aren't there security guards or cameras or something?"

"Right, again. However, the cameras had been disabled during the switching. The guards had been occupied elsewhere. This is a sophisticated operation. And, we think it's getting bigger. The thing is, the thief or mastermind behind this is getting bolder. And, that could be his downfall. Greed is an ugly thing.

"We're thinking the mastermind wants original artwork and likes acquiring paintings that should be hanging in museums. Most of these paintings would never be for sale, anyway. They're strictly museum or high-end private collector artwork. So, he's getting original works for his collection or to sell under the table to some other unscrupulous collector."

"But, they would never be able to display it or tell the world."

"Exactly. But, some collectors don't care about that. They just want what no one else in the world has."

"So, do you think the guy coming with the painting might be involved in this?"

"We don't know. But, what we do know is that this same type of thing happened in a shop in a small town in France about two months ago. A guy calls and says his uncle willed him an ugly painting, and he wants to unload it but doesn't want to auction it off. Says his uncle was a private collector and wouldn't want his name in the press, even though he's dead. We found out about it because the shop owner's sister-in-law is a friend of Ian. She had dinner with the shop owner, her brother-in-law. He was all excited to tell her about maybe having a famous painting in his little shop, but she thought something sounded off and called Ian.

"We came in for the exchange, bought it, and discovered it was a forgery. A really, really good forgery. We're close to knowing exactly where that forger is. Our guys have discovered something on the painting that may be a clue. We're waiting on that. So, even if the one coming here is another forgery, it may help us in getting closer. That's an important piece of the puzzle."

"Okay. So, we're buying it regardless?"

"Probably. Unless it's a complete amateur job. But, the way things are happening, I think we have a connection."

"Okay. Let's hope he shows up. Maybe you can get a better handle on these paintings."

"Suzie, there's one thing I didn't mention yet. And, it might have to do with the car trying to hit you this afternoon as well. The shop owner in France that I mentioned . . ." Pete hesitated and took a sip of wine.

"Yes. What about him?"

"We thought the seller, the guy who called and said his uncle left him the painting, went away happy after he unloaded his painting. Nothing in the whole transaction created a red flag for any of the agents involved. But, a week after our agent was at the shop and bought the painting . . ." Pete sighed and looked directly at Suzie. "The shop owner left his house one morning, started his car like he always did, and it blew up, killing him."

Suzie gulped. "What? What happened?"

"We've been investigating and found pieces and residue of a simple explosive that was probably triggered by him starting his car. Suzie, this is serious business."

Suzie closed her eyes, opened them, and took a sip of wine as Lady nosed her way into Suzie's hand. "Well, hell."

Chapter 18

SUZIE AND PETE left the wine bar, Pete's warnings to be observant and careful floating through Suzie's head as she made her way home. Lady was the perfect lady, sitting in the front seat, watching out the window, and entering the kitchen from the garage when they arrived home.

"I know it's dinnertime, Lady. Let me get the mail, and then we'll eat." Suzie opened the front door to reach into her mailbox, and Lady immediately pushed between Suzie and the door, sniffing and growling. "Hey, what's up? I'm just getting the mail, girl. They told me you had an uncanny nose, and I guess they weren't kidding. What do you smell?" Lady barked and Suzie pulled her hand out of the mailbox, looking around the doorway. Seeing nothing out of the ordinary, Suzie carefully reached into the mailbox and pulled out four pieces of mail.

Bringing them inside, Suzie glanced at them as Lady continued her worried growl. "It's mail. There's a bill from PG&E, one from the alarm company, a flyer from my favorite restaurant, and a cream colored envelope." As she laid them out on the kitchen counter Lady sniffed all of them and singled out the cream envelope, pushing it to the floor. She looked up at Suzie and barked.

"What's up with this one, girl?" Suzie picked it up, saw it was addressed to her, also saw it had no return address, and opened it. A single sheet slid out. "It's an invitation to a party, Lady. But, I don't think you can go. It says Mr. Thomas Smith is having a party to celebrate his aunt's 90th birthday party. Who the hell is Thomas Smith, and why am I invited?" Suzie looked at the address again. "It's addressed to me. But, why? Thomas Smith. Thomas Smith. That's a pretty common name and it doesn't ring any bells with me. I'm going to Google him and see what comes up. I'll probably get a dozen people right here with that name. But, first, I'll feed you, Lady, and then me."

Once Lady was fed and Suzie was eating leftovers with her glass of wine, she looked up Thomas Smith, finding several in the Bay area. "Huh. Here's one who is an art collector, quite wealthy, and a patron of the art scene. Wonder if this is him? But, that still doesn't explain why I was invited to his aunt's birthday party. It says I can bring a guest. Maybe Pete will want to come. Or, Marta. She might be back by then." Lady still seemed upset by the envelope, which was now lying on the counter. "I'd like to know what bothers you about this envelope, Lady. I don't smell anything on it, but it must smell bad to you. I'll shred it so it doesn't bug you anymore. It's late, and we have a couple of big days ahead. Let's go to bed."

Suzie and Lady climbed the grand staircase to her bedroom suite. "I'm glad I have such a large bedroom. That means you have your own space, Lady. Not that you'll stay in your bed, though." Lady woofed, went to her bed, turned around several times, and laid down.

Chapter 19

IN ANOTHER PART of San Francisco, Carlo answered his phone. "Yeah, Boss. It's all set. I'll take the painting to the broad, give her the sob story, collect the money, and leave."

"Once she pays for the painting I want you to do like we discussed, and get your butt back to Italy. You've still got your ticket?"

"Yep. What's going on?"

"Good. I've got some trouble with Serge. First of all, he texted me on my private number, and he knows that is a huge mistake. No one contacts me. I contact them. Then, he's trying to get more money out of me for the forgeries. Finally, he says he's finished painting. That's not going to happen. But, he's starting to threaten me, and I don't take that sitting down." Silently, he thought of what Dixie would do to him if he let Serge quit. Not good.

"Whatcha want me to do when I get there, Boss? Rough him up? Put a bullet in him?"

"No bullets, you idiot. These are my instructions. Go to the apartment in Venice and wait. I'll be in touch with you after I call him. I want you to scare him and remind him who he works for. He thinks he's got the upper hand. He needs to be brought down a couple of notches. Can you handle that?"

"Gotcha. My flight leaves about six hours after I'm done with the broad. Plenty of time to drop the money and head out."

"Good. Remember to act real stupid about the painting and tell her you really need the money. Stay firm in the original price. Got it?"

"Got it. No worries. I'll drop the money where we planned and be gone before dark."

"Okay. Don't screw this up. I need her around for a little longer." He hung up before Carlo could ask what he meant.

Then, he placed another call. "The blonde arrives on a private jet. Here's her address. I want you to hang around and give her a reason to look over her shoulder. You can get close enough to scare her, maybe even run into her. Do whatever you want, but don't let her see you. You know the drill. You'll get your chance to hurt her." Abruptly, he hung up. He tossed that phone in his trash compactor, and grabbed another out of his stash of cheap phone.

Chapter 20

MARIO'S PRIVATE JET with Marta and Shadow on
board had landed in San Francisco. Clark's friend, Stan, a retired
FBI agent, picked them up and headed to her home.

In addition to the villa in Venice, her grandmother left Marta
a significant amount of money. This allowed Marta to trade in her
smallish condo for a home in the affluent Pacific Heights neighborhood. It was considerably larger than she really needed, but
she couldn't pass up the amazing views of the Presidio, the Golden
Gate, and beyond. The quiet neighborhood appealed to her, and
she enjoyed being able to walk through one of the nearby parks.

Recently remodeled, the third story with its perfect office
overlooking the Golden Gate Bridge was one of the main reasons
Marta fell in love with it. That and the chef's kitchen, equipped
for entertaining 50 plus guests or sitting down for a dinner for
one. Approaching her home, Stan motioned to an older model car
sitting down the block, which was completely out of place for this
neighborhood. "Anybody you know?" He gestured toward the dark
sedan with deeply tinted windows.

"Not at all."

"I'll keep an eye out after you go in the house and see what he
does. If it looks funny, I'll call the cops."

"Thanks. I appreciate it." Stan helped Marta carry her things into the house and then sat in her driveway for several minutes. After a couple of minutes, the other car pulled into a driveway down the street, turned around, and sped away. Stan made a call to Clark first and then to the local police, giving the description of the car, including the fact it had no front or rear license plates.

"Shadow, we're finally home. I'm so glad Clark and I had the chance to talk, and I'm excited about thinking of him as my boy-friend. Life is going to get interesting." She sat the carrier down in the foyer, and the perturbed cat walked out, looked around, and immediately began to take a bath. "Let's see if the cleaning service bought the food I asked them to. I'm hungry and you probably are, too. I should call Suzie, but it might be too late. I'll call Clark instead and let him know we're home. It's funny, but I can't wait to talk to him."

After discussing plans to find more time together, Clark filled her in on what they had found in Paris and farther south. "Marta, this is getting more serious by the day. We still aren't sure if every-thing is connected to what's happening in Venice and now in San Francisco. I've called Pete to fill him in on the latest forgeries and murders. Things are getting too close for my comfort level.

"The more I think about your attack in Venice, the more my mind says it was by design. I'm convinced it has to do with the painting you saw. I want you to watch your six at all times. Something's not right. Stan filled me in on the car by your home, and I don't like that either.

"Now, switching gears, will you be able to go to Suzie's shop sometime around noon? If you go, pay close attention to every-thing on the way there. I'd like you to look at the painting as well as visit with them about the transaction. Pete's going to call me when it's all finished. Get some sleep, and I'll talk to you tomorrow."

Marta had slept a bunch on the plane, but she and Shadow were still on Paris time. Even still, she managed to get a few hours, and morning came quickly.

*C*hapter 21

NINE O'CLOCK CAME and went. "Pete, I thought he said nine. What do we do if he doesn't show up?"

As they were talking, Lady perked up her ears, stood up from her bed, and made a low, soft growl.

"It's okay, girl. Oh, remind me to tell you about an invitation I received. Lady didn't like it."

"What about it didn't she like? And, yeah, he did say nine. But, he could be playing us, or he's cautious and savvy, making sure there are no cops of any kind around."

"Are there?"

"We have an agent at the restaurant two doors down. He's sitting by the window, reading the paper. He's changed hats twice and left the restaurant once. He came back wearing different clothes and carrying a laptop. He's a pro. I can't believe he'll be spotted. In fact . . ."

Just as Pete was talking, the front door chimed as it opened, and in walked a tall, muscular, forty-something man dressed in jeans, a Forty-Niner's sweatshirt, a Giants cap pulled down low on his forehead, a black leather jacket, and black leather gloves. Snug up against one side was a brown, square satchel. The other side of his jacket bulged conspicuously. His eyes darted all over as he looked at Suzie, then at Pete, and finally at Lady, who was standing by Suzie's side. "Lady, bed." Lady looked at her, woofed, and laid down in her bed. Suzie came forward, a big smile on her face, her hand outstretched.

"Hello. May I help you? My name is Suzie." She looked him in the eyes, not looking at the cumbersome satchel nor the bulge under his jacket, which bothered her. Silently, she hoped Pete was armed.

Pete had busied himself with another painting towards the back of the shop. He had taken it off the easel, turned it over, put on glasses, and was intently looking at the frame. Lady's ears were at full attention, and she was wound as tight as a spring. Pete dropped his glasses case, reached down to retrieve it, and softly told Lady to be quiet.

The man shifted the satchel a little, looked around, motioned with his head toward Pete, and looked at Lady. "I had an appointment with the owner. Is that you? Is that dog going to bite me?"

"Yes, I am the owner. And, no, the dog won't bite you. Are you the person who called me about a painting that was left to you by your uncle? I'm glad to meet you, Mr. . . ."

"Yeah, that's me. I've got this ugly thing ol' Uncle George left me. I need to get rid of it. Don't want it around anymore. But, someone told me it was worth a fortune. Who's that guy?" He pointed to Pete, who was now examining the front of the painting.

"He's a collector and a special client of mine. Often I give him first shot at new things that come in here. Right now he's looking at a painting I acquired last week. I'm pretty sure he'll buy that one, and I thought he might be a great buyer for your painting. Then again, it might not be something he collects. May I see what you have? We can go to my office. And, I'm sorry. I didn't catch your name." Lady watched intently as Pete watched much more discretely.

The man followed Suzie toward her office, gripping the satchel tighter as they walked past Pete. Finally releasing it, he laid it on Suzie's large work-desk, unclasped the fasteners, and opened the satchel to reveal a Monet. Suzie tried not to gasp, but her heart rate jumped. This wasn't the Renoir she was expecting.

Trying to be professional, Suzie smiled at the man and nodded. "This is nice. Do you know how long your uncle had it?"

"Nope. I just want my money for this thing."

"I don't suppose your uncle left you a provenance or a bill of sale for this?"

"I don't know what those are. I just got this."

"Okay, Mr. . . . Again, I'm sorry I didn't get your name. May I pick it up and look at it? You understand I have to look at a few things before I can offer you the correct amount of money? I need to make sure this is a real Monet." Suzie had put on gloves and a pair of glasses. "Is that okay?"

"My name is not your concern. Go ahead and look at it. Everyone else says it's real."

Suzie thought to herself that that was an odd comment to make, but she didn't say anything about it. She continued to examine the painting, looking for telltale signs. She knew she'd never be able to authenticate it in this short amount of time, but it did look good. Time to call Pete.

"Sir, this is definitely something my client would be interested in owning." She pointed to Pete, in the other room. "If it's okay with you, I'm going to call him in to see this. You might have a quick sale here." She smiled to the man. Her smile was not returned.

"Okay, but no funny business."

"Of course not. I just want to be able to help you. Okay?"

The man nodded as Suzie called to Pete. "Mr. Jensen, will you please come here a minute?"

Pete nodded to the man as he stepped into Suzie's office, gestured to her, and immediately started talking. "I will buy that small piece by the new artist you just discovered. I'd like to take it with me today, if that's okay. It's quite innovative. I know exactly where I'll hang it. I can pay you cash for it. Your asking price is not out of line." He shook his head as if he just remembered Suzie had called him in here.

"Oh. I'm sorry. What did you need?"

"Mr. Jensen, this nice man has a painting his uncle left to him, and he doesn't want it anymore. I thought of you when I saw it. I know you collect Monet." Suzie emphasized the word Monet as Pete looked at her. "If it's not something you want, I know I have other clients who need to see it." She started to say more but was interrupted by the man.

"I just want the money, and you two can decide who gets it." The man shifted from one foot to the other, eyes darting between Suzie and Pete, his hands in and out of his pockets. Pete had noticed the bulge under his jacket when he first entered Suzie's office.

"Certainly. I understand. I'd like Mr. Jensen to look at it, and then I can pay you. Okay?"

Pete's specialty was Monet's works, and this one looked good at first glance. But, he bent over the painting, looking it up and down, not touching a thing. He made a big deal of looking at his watch, then at Suzie and winked ever so slightly. "Miss Suzie, I need to make a quick phone call to cancel another appointment. I'd really like to negotiate with this gentleman on this fine piece."

Pete placed a call, letting the man hear him, and then turned to Suzie. "Okay. Let's talk business. Sir, what kind of money did you have in mind?"

"I need $10,000. In cash. Right now."

Suzie reacted like they had rehearsed. Pete rubbed his chin and nodded.

"That's a little more than I am willing to pay, especially since I haven't had it authenticated yet." Suzie pulled out a notepad and started writing. "I could offer you $7500 right now. That would be a firm offer. But, I certainly don't keep that kind of cash in my shop. You understand that, right? Would you take a check? You can call the bank to verify I'm good for it."

"No check. Cash. And, I'd take $8000, but that's as low as I can go."

She looked at the painting again. "Hmmm. I'll give you $8000, but I need to go to the bank if you really want cash. And, I need to call in another expert to verify if it's a genuine Monet. Can you come back in an hour or so?"

"No. I need the money now. Maybe I should just leave."

Pete looked up from his examination of the painting. "I have that much cash on me. Why don't I pay for it? I want it anyway."

"You carry that much cash on you? And, you'd buy it without it being thoroughly checked out?" Suzie stared at Pete. She started to say more but was interrupted by the guy.

"Fine. Let's do this." The man was getting more nervous as the minutes ticked by. "I'll take the cash now, and you can have the damn thing. I already told you, it's real."

Chapter 22

PETE STEPPED OUT of Suzie's office and pulled out his wallet, while the man nervously looked from Suzie to Pete to the floor. Suzie tried to make small talk. "I'm glad your uncle left this to you. And I'm glad you found my shop. It all works out, huh? You gain some money, and this collector gains a piece. Do you have plans for the rest of the day? It looks like it will be sunny and nice."

The man ignored Suzie's attempts to put him at ease, looking instead at his watch, jamming his hands into his pockets, and moving around Suzie's office. "How long does it take him to count out the money? I need to go. Got a plane to catch." The minute he said that, his eyes widened, and his breath quickened. "I mean I got an appointment for lunch."

Suzie nodded, noticing the comment, but didn't say anything about it. She looked down at the painting, her back to the man. "Yes, I'm getting hungry, too. I'm sure Mr. Jensen is just making sure he counts the money correctly. As a word of caution, I wouldn't walk around with that much cash on you. You never know what could happen. You are taking it to the bank, aren't you?"

He didn't answer.

"This is a very nice painting. I'm sure Mr. Jensen will be so pleased with it." She still had on her gloves and smoothed out the brown paper under the painting. She was running out of things to say, especially since this was a one-sided conversation. She looked up at him. "I need to get a bill of sale for you. How do you want it made out?"

He still didn't answer, but instead shoved his hands back into his pocket.

Pete came back with a stack of crisp, $100 bills in his hand. "These are so crisp, I needed to make sure I didn't short change you. It's been a pleasure doing business with you." He counted out $8,000 for the man, who folded the stack and stuffed them inside his jacket and turned to leave, never saying a word. He didn't shake Pete's outstretched hand.

Suzie caught up with him by the front door. "Thank you so much for bringing the painting here. Oh, I never asked you how you decided on my shop. Did someone refer you? If so, I'd like to thank them."

Lady barked from the back of the shop, and Pete reached down to pet her.

"Sure. Whatever. I just saw your name, that's all." With that strange exchange, he grabbed the front door handle just as Marta entered. Startled, he shoved past her while quickly leaving the shop, and disappeared around the corner. Marta glanced nervously over her shoulder, up and down the street, before she entered.

$\mathcal{C}$hapter 23

"WHOA. WAS THAT the guy with the Renoir?" Marta asked as she walked into Suzie's shop and looked over her shoulder again at the space where the exiting man had been.

"Hello, Marta. Sorry about that. Did he hurt you? You look a little nervous. Are you okay?"

"I'm fine. And, no he didn't hurt me. I'm just paying attention to a car that's been following me. It's the same car that was sitting outside my house last night, or at least it looks like it. This guy startled me; that's all. Now, where is the Renoir?"

"Well, funny thing. He brought the painting and was in an awful hurry to leave once he had his money. I didn't even have a chance to write a bill of sale. But, even stranger . . . it's not a Renoir. It's a Monet."

"A Monet?"

Pete had come up behind Suzie, finishing his phone conversation. He looked at Suzie. "I just gave the guy's description to our agent down the street. He and a couple of SFPD spotted him and are tailing him. We'll see what happens with that. He was on foot, constantly looking over his shoulder. He seemed to be heading toward the Russian Hill area. Kind of strange." Pete looked from Suzie to Marta. "You must be Marta."

Suzie interrupted. "Pete, yes this is Marta Swenson. Marta, meet Pete Jensen. Whew! It's been quite the morning." Lady nosed her face into Marta's hand. "And, this is Lady. She didn't seem to like that guy very much."

"Hello, Lady. Apparently, you have good taste. How long have you had her?" Marta was scratching Lady's ears.

"Only a couple of days, and she's already become my hero. I'll explain later."

Marta nodded at Pete. "So, a Monet, huh? May I see it?"

As they walked to the back of the shop and entered Suzie's office, Marta looked at the painting lying on the table, and turned to Suzie with a puzzled look on her face. "This is a surprise, isn't it?"

Pete spoke up. "Right. We were both surprised when he unwrapped this one. Not sure what's going on. Everything else was exactly as he said on the phone. Maybe he has another painting, or he doesn't know a Renoir from a Monet. As for this one, it will be inspected at our lab for fingerprints, dating, and so on. It may be a forgery, but if so, it's a good one. We haven't touched anything, as Suzie had her gloves on the whole time. Not sure it we'll get any other fingerprints off anything, especially if this is a pro job. He was wearing gloves, probably the whole time he handled it.

"I've already called Ian and left a voicemail. Suzie, we both need to verbalize what we saw and heard from this guy now before we forget any details. Marta, why don't you listen as we tell you what happened, and you can ask questions when we're finished. Okay? We'll record it. Suzie, can we lock the shop so no one else comes in? The officers or our agent will call before they come here. No sense spooking anyone who might be watching the shop."

"You think somebody is watching?"

"You never know in cases like this. I'm just covering all possibilities."

About twenty minutes later, Pete and Suzie had finished talking, filling in details of the transaction. Marta had been taking notes and had a few questions. When most of those were answered, she had one more. "Suzie, don't you have some type of security camera we could look at?"

Pete was the one who answered. "Yes, she does. Sorry for answering, Suzie. I didn't want us to look at it until after we had recalled what we could from the meeting. It will corroborate what we've seen, and it may now cause us to remember something else. Let's look at it."

Suzie pulled it up on her computer, and all three watched as the man came into the first screen, standing at the front door. "He's talking on his phone. How long was he out there?"

Pete watched as he stood there, and then played that part again. "He's definitely on his phone, but it's hard to tell if he's actually talking or just listening. When we're done here, I need to give this to our guys to inspect every detail. Let's keep watching."

Nothing else jumped out at the three of them, until he was moving around Suzie's office while waiting to be paid. They could see Suzie making small talk and see him walking around the table while Suzie was looking down at the painting. "Wait. Stop it. Right there. See that?" Pete motioned to the screen.

Marta saw it before Suzie. "It looks like he dropped something into your bag, Suzie, while you were looking down, and Pete wasn't in the room." Marta motioned to Suzie's oversized black and white patterned bag sitting on the floor.

"She's right. His perceived nervousness was to distract you, Suzie. Let me look in the bag. We don't want any more fingerprints."

"I can put my gloves back on and look." Pete nodded as Suzie put on her gloves and carefully opened the top of her bag. "I never zip it shut. Guess I'll have to start."

"He would have found somewhere else to leave something. Can you take out everything that's in there and put it here on this desk?"

"Sure. Here goes. You guys are going to see all my daily treasures."

Chapter 24

AS SUZIE EMPTIED her bag, Lady stuck her nose in and then pawed at the bag. "Well, she thinks she found something. I'm going to slowly dump everything out to see if we can figure out what she found."

A red, leather wallet, a small, red bag with make-up, a folder with some paperwork, a set of keys, two granola bars, a few tissues, a crumpled up receipt for dry cleaning, two pens, her cell phone, and a re-sealable bag with dog treats slid onto the desk. Suzie set the bag back on the floor. "Nothing that looks out of place to me."

Lady nudged her whole head into the bag and growled. Pete picked up the bag and opened it with one of the tissues. Lady stood on her hind feet to help him.

"Down, girl. Let him look." Suzie motioned for her to come to her side.

"Aha. We're right, and so is Lady. He did put something in here. Let me have a glove, Suzie."

Carefully, Pete reached in with a gloved hand and pulled out a tiny, round piece.

"It looks like a small battery. What is it?"

"I'd bet it's a tracking device of some type, Suzie. Do you have an envelope to put this in? Our guys need this ASAP." Pete was already on the phone.

Suzie hugged Lady. "What's going on? I don't get it. Why track me?"

"We have an agent coming here in a couple of minutes. Why don't you unlock the front door so he can come in? He'll look like a client in case we're still being watched. Do you have a back door?"

"Yeah, it goes into the alley. But won't they be watching that, too?"

"Probably not. He'll stay a while and then decide how he wants to leave. Earlier you mentioned an invitation. What's that about?"

Suzie filled Pete and Marta in on how Lady barked and growled at the invitation. "It's just an invitation to a party. I don't even know the guy. Here, it's in my folder of papers." She pulled it out and showed it to them. "I have no idea why Lady growled at it either. I mean the shelter told me she had a fantastic nose . . . but this is beyond fantastic, if you ask me."

Marta read it over, a puzzled look on her face.

"You're positive you don't know him, Suzie? Has he ever come into your shop or bought something from you?"

"I don't think so, but let me look at my clients." Suzie sat down at the computer and pulled up her database of clients. "Nope. He's not here at all."

"It's curious the way Lady reacted to that piece of paper and now to this bug. It's almost like she knows something's not right. Hmm. It looks like the party is next weekend. I think you should go and check it out. Marta, can you go with Suzie? I don't want to show up and have someone recognize me. If there is something funny going on, we wouldn't want to tip anyone's hand. Oh, there's your front door, Suzie. Maybe it's our agent."

Chapter 25

"AGENT STU THOMPSON, good to see you again. This is Suzie, the shop owner and receiver of the bug I mentioned. Were you involved in tailing our guy?" Pete had answered the door.

He shook Suzie's hand and smiled at her. "Call me Stu." Looking at Pete, he said "No, I wasn't. I've been about a block away at a sidewalk café, just watching the action. At this point I don't think anyone else is watching the shop. At least not close by. We could always have someone who's looking longer distance, but now that we know there's a bug, probably not. Let's see what you've got."

Pete handed the bag to Stu, who took a quick look. "Yep, it's a bug. But, not all that fancy or sophisticated. Wonder why? Any idea what you did to have somebody think they needed to keep tabs on you, Suzie?"

She shook her head. "Not at all. I lead a fairly boring life. Or, at least, I did lead a fairly boring life before I sold that forgery to the Ascots."

Pete turned and looked at her. "What do you mean, a forgery? Who are the Ascots? I think we'd better start at the beginning."

Marta and Lady had come to the front just as Pete was suggesting they all go sit down and hear what Suzie had to say. Lady sniffed Agent Thompson and wagged her tail.

"Suzie, please back up and tell us how you came to sell a forgery."

Suzie filled them in on the fiasco of the Ascot's Picasso.

"Long story, but in the end it was a forgery that was being sold as an original. Marta was the one who noticed some color issues. Apparently, the auctioneer was in on some scam, and it was a huge mess. Bottom line, I needed to get it back from the Ascots, so it could go to the authorities. But, before I could contact them, it disappeared from their home.

"Funny thing about the auctioneer, too. He disappeared and no one has heard from him. It's so confusing."

"Where was the auction?"

"At an invitation-only auction in Carmel, Stu. It's a legitimate auction company, and they have sales there once a year. I had never gone before, as things can get real pricey there. This time I went because the Ascots were looking for a painting by Picasso, and I saw this one listed. I felt lucky to be able to purchase it for them. Now it's gone, and I'm in the middle of another mess."

Chapter 26

AFTER CARLO LEFT Suzie's shop, he headed toward the park in the Russian Hill area. His phone rang. "Yeah, Boss. It's all done. I got the $8,000 for it, and I dropped the bug in her bag. You'll be able to track her now. I'm just about to the spot to drop the cash.

"What? Yeah, sure. I can take it to the airport instead and leave it in the locker. No problem. Why the change of plans? No, just curious, that's all. I'll do it. Yeah, yeah, all the money will be there. It's cash, just like you wanted. Everything's good. No tail." He nodded at the phone.

"Okay? I told you, I really don't think I'm being followed. I've been careful and haven't seen any cops or anyone else around. In fact, I was just about to sit and have a cup of coffee. No, I already told you I'm not being followed. Trust me." Frowning at his phone, he looked around.

"I said, I got it. Stop worrying. It's going according to plan." He gestured with his phone, shook his head, and tried to keep his voice low. He really wanted to yell at the man on the other end.

"I'm good. I'll just grab a cab and head to the airport. The money will be in the locker in the International Terminal, just like before. Yeah, I know where it is. No, the cabbie won't recognize me. I've already changed clothes. I know what I'm doing. You don't have to remind me, so stop worrying.

"What? Okay. I'll touch base once I'm in Venice. I'll give Serge a reason to play nice. Talk to you later. Yeah, I've got it. Don't worry about me."

Carlo hung up, his frown deepening. "That guy is beginning to bug me. He second guesses everything I do, like I can't think for myself. He's not even the real boss. She is. He's just a loser."

Chapter 27

ANOTHER MAN ENTERED Suzie's shop. Agent Thompson nodded and introduced him to everyone. "This is Roger, from our lab. He's going to look at the bug and then take the painting you just purchased to our lab."

After greeting everyone, Roger put on gloves, took the bug out of the plastic bag, and inspected it. In a couple of minutes, he came out of Suzie's office to where the rest were talking about the invitation. "I've dusted this for fingerprints, and nothing showed up. This bug is not too terribly sophisticated. It's basically just a GPS. It doesn't record or do anything other than let the person on the other end know where you are. When I take the painting and the satchel, I'll dust those for fingerprints as well. Did anyone here touch anything?"

Pete looked at Roger. "Nope. Suzie wore gloves the whole time, and I didn't touch anything. You might be able to pull fingerprints off the satchel if he wasn't wearing his gloves at some point. Why don't we put all of it in another package for you? That way, if anyone is watching, they'll think you bought something. Back to the bug, I'm thinking we want to keep it here and not send it to the lab. No sense letting someone know we're on to them."

"Good idea, Pete. What's the life of these things, Roger?"

"Well, it's hard to say. Since he dropped it in her bag, he expects to follow her for a while. But, he also risks having something heavy dropped in the bag and affecting its usefulness."

"I think we leave her bag and the bug here in the shop. Suzie, can you use a different bag?"

"Sure. No problem. In fact, I don't like having that thing with me, anyway. I have plenty of bags I can use. But, won't that person know something isn't right? I mean, it's not like I stay here 24/7."

"He might. And, he's more apt to think you've switched bags than found the bug. I don't want to scare you, but I also want to impress upon you that this is serious. He may be watching this shop or your home or both. If that's the case, you should use a different, large colorful bag every day so he sees that. If it's the same guy who dropped in the bug that's following you, he may or may not remember this bag is black and white. If he does remember, he'll just think you change your bag daily. That won't set off any red flags to him. Okay?"

"I can do that. But, you are scaring me. Why me? Do I have something else he wants?"

Agent Thompson and Pete looked at each other.

"What? What's going on?" Suzie looked from one to the other. Marta sighed.

Pete looked at Marta. "Did Clark or Ian fill you in on what's been going on in France?"

"A little bit. And, some of it reminds me of this scenario. But, I don't understand the connection. Suzie hasn't been in France, and her paintings didn't come from there. So, what's up?"

"We think some of it stems from Italy, as well. One of the crates in which one of forgeries came had a bunch of dirt and some dried weeds that are typically found in the hills north of Venice. Don't ask me how it was traced to there. That's out of my scope. I just know it's causing suspicion. A whole lot of suspicion."

"But, Pete, I still don't get the connection to here and to Suzie."

"Interpol has discovered some correspondence leading them to believe people behind the forgeries and murders in France live here in San Francisco."

"Murders?" Suzie's face went pale as she hugged Lady.

Chapter 28

AGENT THOMPSON'S PHONE rang, and he stepped away. Pete and Roger wrapped up the painting and its satchel, placing it in a brown, non-descript box. Marta sat by Suzie, and Lady had her head in Suzie's lap.

"Marta, why me? How did I get involved in this? Do you think it's somebody I know? It all started with that damn painting I bought in Carmel, didn't it? Does that mean the Ascots are involved, too? They're such a sweet, old couple. I can't believe they'd be involved. They can't be involved. They lost a lot of money on it. I'm sorry. I'm not making any sense."

"I have no answers for you. But, maybe Pete or Stu do."

Pete and Roger came to where the two women and Lady were sitting. "Roger is going to leave by way of the front door. His van is outside, and if anyone is watching, it will just look like he's picking up a piece of artwork. The lab will do its things and tell us what we've got here.

"The bug is going to stay here in your bag. Stu will be leaving to conference in with Ian and Clark. We don't know what's been happening in France in the last day or so. I'm supposed to leave for Italy tonight, but I'll be back in a week. I hate to leave you both, but I really need to check with a contact in the Venice area. Everything keeps pointing to there.

"I'd like for you to run 'business as usual' here in the shop, Suzie, in case they do have somebody watching you. Will that be a problem? We're putting agents in the area to keep an eye on things in the neighborhood. You won't see them, but they'll be around.

"Marta, Clark told me about your attack. Anything else happen to you in the last few days?"

"What attack, Marta?"

Marta first told them about the man who grabbed her in Venice, glossing over the seriousness of it so she wouldn't upset Suzie. "I'm organizing my next trip to Italy. It's an art trip to Venice and the lagoon islands. It's a full trip, and we leave a little over two weeks from today. I was scouting out additional galleries, shops, and museums in Venice for that trip before I came home. Basically, the details are finalized, and I'm just wrapping up last minute things. Clark doesn't know if any of that is connected to the guy that grabbed me. Since I've been back, there's a strange car I've been seeing, almost like it's following me. It's something that worries Clark."

"Okay. Keep your eyes open, Marta."

Stu stuck his phone back in his pocket, waved goodbye to Roger, and came into Suzie's office. He gave Lady a pat on the head. "Well, things are heating up in France. There's been another murder connected with yet another auction house. It seems whoever is spearheading all these sales of forgeries is tying up loose ends. There's no one left that has seen anyone connected to these paintings. The small houses are becoming paranoid and rightly so. Many of them have cancelled their upcoming sales.

"The good news is, Ian is getting closer to figuring out where the forgeries are being done. His lab traced some more pieces, the crates I think, to Italy. Aren't you headed to Italy, Pete?"

"Yeah, tonight. What can you tell me?"

"Apparently, some packing material that was used consisted of old papers in with the foam and bubble wrap stuff. This same material has been found in four of the auction houses where the murders occurred. All the papers point to a small town north of Venice. Plus, they're in the process of trying to figure out a small symbol found near the signature. It's puzzling right now."

"Did you say papers?"

"Yeah, Pete. I haven't seen them, but Ian said they reminded him of newsprint weight paper, some blank, all shredded, and tied into bundles. Like they were meant to be used as packing. But, our lab guys took them all apart, pieced them back together, and found names of businesses. They're sending the specifics to your secure email so you'll have them when you get there. I'll let Ian fill you in on what they want.

"In the meantime, I need to get back. Roger will let us know as soon as the lab knows something about that painting. Suzie, we have an agent who will be in the neighborhood and one who will be near your home. Keep your eyes open at all times. I'm glad you've got this watchdog. I'll be in touch."

Chapter 29

IN ITALY, SERGE had another disturbing voicemail, including more threats. They definitely were escalating in frequency and becoming more graphic. He shuddered as he listened, then walked out to his garden where Harry was working. "Harry, I want you to listen to this voicemail and let me know what you think."

Harry took the phone, listened as his eyes widened, and he handed phone back to Serge. "Whoa, man. That's some nasty words. Who the hell does this guy think he is, anyway? You need to be done with him ASAP. What are you going to do?"

"That's just it. Yesterday I told him I'm done painting and that he'll get the ones I have, including his rush job. I also told him I was moving on to other things, figuring he'd understand. But, you heard what he said. Why does he think he can bully me and threaten me? Why does he call the shots and tell me what to do and when to do it? Do you think he'd really go to the police? I don't want to end up in jail."

"I'd be more concerned about those last threats, if I was you. Those are serious, man."

"Yeah. You're right. Those bother me more than the others."

"Have you ever met him?"

"Nope. I don't even know what this guy looks like. When he sends for the paintings, he has a different courier come each time, and every one of them is a big guy. They all look like thugs."

"This is bad, Serge. Maybe you should go to the police first. You kept all his voicemails, right? I'd think they would be interested in hearing those threats."

"Yeah, I kept them all. Maybe the police would listen. Besides, in the last month I have been doing a couple of things that maybe would help me."

"Really? Like what?"

"Well, nobody knows this but me. And, now you. Under the paint, right by the artist's signature, I painted a small key. Most people won't even see it, as it's real faint. If a real art expert is looking at it, or if it ends up in some high end lab, they could find it easily with their special lights."

"A key? What kind of a key?"

"An old key, like one you'd use to open an antique door. You know, the ones that look like a long piece with some circles on top."

"You mean, something like a skeleton key?"

"Yeah. I paint them all the same and put them right by the signature in hopes somebody will think to look at the painting more closely. It's all I could think of and over the last six or eight months, I've painted it in every single one, even the small ones.

"I've also put some shredded paper from the mill here in town inside the crates. The company's name is on the paper, but it wouldn't look suspicious to anyone. It just looks like packing paper. And, I started putting some grass and dirt inside the crates. Again, I don't know if anyone will notice. But, it's worth a try. I have to do something. I can't keep doing this, Harry. I want out. I'm desperate."

"I've always wondered why and how you got started forging paintings. You're such a great artist. It seems like a shame."

"I was in college, sitting in a bar." Serge sighed as he remembered the meeting like it was yesterday. "I had just been to a lecture on how Interpol agents catch thieves, and I decided I wanted to be one of those agents. While I was figuring out how to transition out of art history and into the criminal justice field, I was drawing in my sketchbook for an art class. A guy came up to me and told me I had talent. He bought that sketch for a huge amount of money. I was in Heaven.

"He came back the next night and told me I could make bigger bucks working for his boss. Well, what college student wouldn't want that? All I had to do was draw and paint. A no brainer in my estimation. I could make enough to switch majors and go into criminal justice. In fact, the money was fantastic to a poor college student like me. He even set me up in a studio and told me what to paint. A few funny thoughts kept creeping in. But, damn, that money was good. So, I painted. And, I painted.

"He kept coming and giving me money. At some point I told him I was done and needed to get on with college." Serge let out a huge breath.

"What happened?"

"This big guy showed up and beat me up pretty good. He told me that if I went to the cops, his boss would tell them I was a forger, and I'd rot in jail."

"That's blackmail, Serge. They can't do that."

"I know that now. At the time, I was scared to death. So, I kept painting. I finished college and moved up here. But, they found me. I was beat up again and told to paint or else my grandpa's wine business would be burned. By this time, I had probably forged twenty paintings. I felt trapped and scared.

"It's only in the last few months that I've gathered enough gumption to take him on. Whoever he is. I still don't even know his name. Or where he lives. Or anything about him."

"What do they do with the paintings?"

"I think they must sell them. That's why I started painting the little key under just one layer of paint. It's my only hope at this point."

"Okay. Let's figure out how to get you out of this mess. We're both smart. We just need to outsmart the bad guys. I need to leave right now for another appointment, but let's meet at my place the day after tomorrow. You don't have a courier coming before then, do you?"

"No. He's not due for another week." Serge smiled at Harry. "Thanks for listening and for helping me. I'll see you in a couple of days. Thanks again."

"No problem, man. We'll figure this out."

Serge started to wave to Harry and then called him back. "Hey, Harry. Will you do a favor for me?"

"Sure. What do you need?"

"I had this strange dream again, and I want to get this last crate of paintings out of here. I really don't expect the courier for a week, but something is bothering me. If those paintings aren't here, I'll feel better. You don't need to keep them at your house. Why don't you put them in the back room at the bar? Sylvie will let you if you tell her I'm just storing them for a couple of days."

"I'll take them home. Don't worry. We'll get to the bottom of this and clear your name. See ya in two days."

Chapter 30

JUST AS STU and Pete were ready to leave Suzie's shop in San Francisco, Stu's phone rang. When he hung up, he shook his head. "Our guys lost him."

"What? How?"

"Well, they were taking turns with some local guys, and no one knows how or where he vanished. But, he's gone."

"That's not good."

"No kidding. I'm going to fill our guys in and ask them to pay close attention to you and your shop, Suzie. I want both of you to keep your eyes and ears open at all times. We don't need anything to happen to either one of you." He looked at both Suzie and Marta, but didn't mention to Suzie that she was the only shop owner still alive that had seen someone selling a forgery. His gut twisted at the thought.

"Do I need to leave and go somewhere else?"

Pete and Stu looked at each other. "Probably not, Suzie. But, is there anyone who can stay with you? I know you have a great watchdog, but it wouldn't hurt to have another person around."

"Suzie can stay with me. My cat, Shadow, might not like Lady right away. But, he'll just have to get used to her."

"Thanks, Marta. But, is it really necessary for me to go to all this trouble?"

Pete sat down next to Suzie. "I think it's a good idea for you to stay with Marta for a week or so, especially with this guy on the loose. We don't want him coming back here. And, we are so close to figuring out what's going on. Somehow all of these forgeries are connected, and it appears they all lead to Italy. I'll know more once I can look at what's going on from there. If the next week is uneventful, then you can move back home. Okay?"

Plans were discussed, and Pete gave names and numbers of the agents to Suzie and Marta. "Don't hesitate to call any one of these people. Okay? I'll check in with you every day and see how things are going here." With that, everyone left Suzie's shop except for Suzie and Marta.

"I need to get home, Suzie, and make some phone calls. Why don't you come whenever you finish up here?"

"Sure thing. I want to take Lady for a run on the beach. I think we're both a little stressed out right now. I'll probably be there in two hours or so. Will that work?"

"Sounds good. Even though it's still daylight, be careful." Marta headed to the front door.

"I will. After our run, we'll stop by home, grab some things, and raid my wine cellar. Bye." Suzie waited until everyone was gone and wandered through her shop. "I wonder if I have any other forgeries, Lady. Now, I'm being paranoid. Let's get our stuff together, stop at home to change, and go for a run. Okay?"

Lady wagged her tail as they headed out the front door and to the parking garage. Suzie did as Pete told her to and paid close attention to people and cars. As she and Lady exited the garage and headed toward home, she thought she saw a dark blue SUV following her. Twice she looked in the rear view mirror and saw the same vehicle. She was about to stop and call one of the agents when the SUV turned a corner and headed in a different direction. "Okay. Stop being spooked." She spoke out loud as Lady looked at her.

Chapter 31

ONCE SUZIE HAD changed, she and Lady headed to Ocean Beach. "I have no idea if you like the water or not, but this a good beach to run off some energy, Lady." She attached her leash, and they jogged and walked for about an hour.

"Whew. That felt good, huh girl? Let's go home, get cleaned up, and go to Marta's. You get to meet a kitty. We'll see how that goes." Lady shook off the sand as they walked back to Suzie's car. When they were close enough, Suzie hit the button to unlock it and was about to take off Lady's leash when Lady stopped in her tracks, sniffed the air, and started growling.

Suzie immediately looked around. "What is it? What did I miss, Lady?" Nothing looked out of the ordinary. No one else was on the beach or in the parking lot. She bent down to talk to Lady, still looking all around. Nothing.

Standing up, she took off the leash and walked toward her car. Lady pushed her way in front of her, now barking. "What's up? What do you see? Do you smell something?" The barking increased. "Okay. I won't go near the car. You seem to know what you're doing, and every time you bark like this, something isn't quite right." She pulled her phone out of her pocket and dialed one of the agents.

With Lady's leash back on, they walked to a bench to wait, Lady still growling softly. A dark sedan pulled up, and a man in jeans and sweatshirt got out. Lady quit growling, so Suzie figured he must be okay.

"Hi, I'm Agent Jon Hansen. Please call me Jon. Stu said you would call if you had a problem? What's going on?" As he introduced himself to Suzie and pet Lady, he looked all around. "Did you see something?"

"Agent Hansen, Jon, we've been here for a little over an hour and were just about to get back in my car to go home. Lady wouldn't let me go near it, barking and growling. I've already unlocked it with my key fob, but that's all the farther I got. I have no idea if something's wrong, but Agent Thompson and Pete made me a little paranoid, especially after that car almost hit me. If there's nothing, I apologize." Suzie stood up with Lady by her side.

"Let's walk toward the car a couple of steps and see what she does." They took one step, Lady whined and then barked. "Okay. Far enough. I've been around a lot of trained police dogs and know enough that they sense things we don't. Something is bothering her. Why don't you sit back down, and I'm going to call in a couple of guys?"

Chapter 32

TWO MORE CARS with three agents arrived. Once they talked to Agent Hansen, two of the new agents and Agent Hansen came to the bench where Suzie and Lady were sitting. He introduced them and told Suzie the plan.

"Agent Carillo is putting on special gear, and then he's going to inspect your car, Suzie. We all need to move down the beach a little."

"Why? What does he think is in my car? It was locked the whole time we were here. I double checked."

"It's not so much what's in it, but he'll be looking for something that could have been placed on the outside of it. Did you have the car in sight the whole time you were here?"

"Not really. We walked and ran down the beach quite a ways, maybe a mile or more. And, my back would have been to the car during that time. The only people were way down there; two guys and a girl were playing with a Frisbee. They had a shepherd of some type that was trying to catch it. We waved and commented on each other's dogs. But, that's all I saw."

"Okay. Let's move. Agent Carillo is ready." Agent Hansen motioned to another bench down the beach. "Let's go there."

They all watched as Agent Carillo, in his big, rubber-like suit and helmet walked toward the car. In his hand was something that looked like a small computer tablet and a long handled tool. "What's he doing?"

"He's checking for anything that would leave residue, and he's looking under the car for something that doesn't belong there."

"You mean, like a bomb?"

"Well, yes, but that's only one option. Let's not jump to conclusions just yet. It may be something that Lady didn't like the smell of as well."

"Don't you use robots to find things like this? Or, is that just in the movies?"

"Yes, we do use robots. We just didn't have time to get one here. And, Agent Carillo is a retired Army bomb specialist." Realizing he might upset Suzie further, he added. "That just means he knows what he's doing. It doesn't mean we're dealing with a bomb. Let's see what he has to say." Agent Carillo had worked his way around the car, and now had taken off his mask and helmet, and was headed toward the group.

He motioned toward Agent Hansen. "You're going to want to get this to the lab. I've disabled it, but they're going to want it. Looks like we're dealing with someone who doesn't want you around." He looked at Suzie.

"What is it?"

Agent Hansen put on gloves, took the device, and looked at it. "Suzie, it appears this is a device that was meant to blow up your car. You're lucky it wasn't triggered by your remote when you unlocked your car. You're also lucky you have this great nose." He pointed to Lady, who was growling at his hand. "She really doesn't like this." He pulled out a bag and sealed the device into it.

"Is my car safe now? How do I know?"

Agent Carillo was taking off his padded jacket. "Ma'am, this is a simple device rigged to go off once your car had moved a few feet. Starting it wouldn't have done anything. But, moving it would have. I checked everything else on and around your car, and nothing else is a problem. You're good to go. We can even take your car home if that would make you feel better. You could ride with one of us."

Agent Hansen agreed. "Good idea. But, we need to all be extra careful. If the guy who planted this is watching, he already knows we found it. If he's too far away to see what's going on, he's waiting for a big boom. When that doesn't happen, he's going to get upset. Who knows what he'll try to do. This guy is serious."

"I was going to go home, pick up some things, and head to Marta's house. She's a friend of Clark, Ian, and I'm not sure who else. Should I still do that?"

"I know both Clark and Ian, and that's a good idea to stay with someone else. But, again, if we're being watched, he'll know where you are."

Agent Carillo looked at Suzie and Agent Hansen. "We have four vehicles here. He can't possibly be watching all of us. Ours have dark windows, so he couldn't see which one we're in. Let's think this through."

Chapter 33

ONCE THE PLAN was finalized, it was decided that Agent Hansen would wear Suzie's hat, drive her car home, and put it in her garage for a few minutes. He would then drive back out and to a parking ramp by Ghirardelli Square, watching to see if anyone was following him. After an hour or so he would drive back to her home and would stay in Suzie's house that night.

Agent Greg Mitchell, with Suzie and Lady, would also drive to her home and drive into the garage after Agent Hansen left. The windows were dark enough that no one would be able to tell who was in the car. Finally, the last agent would head away from the beach, but circle back and watch Suzie's home from a distance. He would let Agent Hansen know if anyone had followed the car with Suzie in it.

Once Suzie had everything she needed to go to Marta's, she and Lady would then leave with the agent. Again, no one would be able to see who was in the SUV. They all had their instructions and set off to complete the plan. Suzie was nervous and on edge. "I don't understand what's going on. Why me? How long is this guy going to keep coming after me?" Agent Mitchell shook his head and then turned toward Suzie.

"I can't answer those questions. I know Ian is positive this is all connected to a huge forgery ring. Pete will be back in a couple of days, and he'll stay with you until things settle down. Right now, you need to stay focused on your surroundings. And, pay attention to this great dog. Where'd you get her, anyway? Is she a trained police dog or something?"

"I just got her two days ago, but it seems like she's always been with me. She had come to the shelter when her owner, an elderly woman, had died. The manager of the shelter is going to get back to me with more of her history. They know she's about two years old and told me she has a terrific nose. Actually, I had gone there hoping to get a little lap dog to keep me company at home and at the shop. I thought a big dog would be too much trouble.

"Boy, am I glad they showed Lady to me. It was love at first sight, for both of us. Now that you mention it, she does seem to act like she's had some training. I'll be sure to ask them when they call. She's awfully smart, and she seems to recognize danger pretty quickly. I wonder why."

"Maybe she was trained to watch the old lady, her former owner. She seems like a natural."

His phone buzzed, and he talked to Agent Hansen. Nodding, he hung up. "Okay, Suzie. Jon is positive he's been followed to and from your home. He saw a vehicle and so did one of the under-cover agents who was following. He lost him now, which was the idea. He'll finish the plan and go back to your house in about an hour. We haven't been followed at all, so let's head to your house, get your things, and then go to Marta's. Please let her know we need to drive into her garage."

Suzie grabbed what she thought she would need from home and then called Marta to let her know they were on their way. Once there, Marta's garage door opened and closed as they pulled in and got out of his car. Agent Mitchell introduced himself to Marta as she met them in the garage. "Call me Greg. I'm positive no one followed us, but I'm going to call our agent who should be watching in this neighborhood."

Once he got off the phone, he smiled at the two. "All's clear."

"Well, Greg, it's a pretty calm neighborhood. However, I swear I was again followed on my way home. I even went around a couple of blocks to make sure. The same dark blue car followed me, closer than I like, until I made the last turn. Then, it went a different direction. Clark told me to pay attention, and this one stuck out big time. In fact, I'm sure it was the same car we saw sitting down the block last night."

Greg made a note of it as Marta was talking. "Did you get any numbers on the license plate?"

"No. In fact I'm almost certain there was no front license plate." Smiling at Suzie, Marta motioned for them all to go inside. "Let's introduce Lady to Shadow. This should be interesting."

Chapter 34

SHADOW WAS SITTING on the top step watching the group come into the house from the garage. Lady, still on her leash, noticed him right away, her tail wagging.

"Here, Suzie, let me lead Lady to Shadow and see what he does. Hopefully, she won't chase him. This could go okay or really, really badly." Marta took Lady and walked slowly up the stairs, talking to Shadow the whole time. Lady sniffed, her tail wagging on double speed. Shadow stood up, full arch of his back, tail fluffed to the maximum, raised a paw, and tapped Lady on the nose. Claws were not out, so no damage was done. What happened next, surprised all of them.

Lady lay down on the top step, next to Shadow, with her belly exposed, and legs in the air. Shadow rubbed her head with his. Then Lady flipped over, and followed Shadow down the stairs, never making a sound.

"What the hell?" Greg shook his head. "I've never seen a big dog follow a cat before. Although, that's a pretty big cat. What's up with that?"

Marta had taken the leash off Lady, and the two animals were walking around the ground floor like they had been best friends for decades. "Well, this happened with a friend's husky in England. He thought of Shadow as the Alpha and followed him all over.

Maybe Lady has enough husky in her to have that same pack mentality. Apparently, Shadow is the Alpha around here. Go figure.

"Now that they're doing okay, let's get you settled, Suzie. Greg, you can fill me in on what's going on."

Once Marta had the whole story, she nodded. "What do we do? Do you think I'm being watched as well? Is the car that's been following me connected? Could it have something to with my attack in Venice?" She started to sit down and jumped up. "Oh, I almost forgot. Guess what came in the mail. It is addressed to me, but has the wrong house number so it went to my neighbor. He noticed my name and didn't open it. He just brought it to me today and doesn't really remember when it was originally delivered." Marta brought a cream colored envelope into the den, where they were sitting.

"Is that what I think it is?" Suzie reached for the envelope.

"Yep. It's an invitation to the same party." She filled Greg in on what Pete and Ian thought. "Neither Suzie nor I know this guy, so who knows why we both received invitations."

"Does Ian think you should go?"

"Yes, he does. I was originally going to go as Suzie's date. Pete didn't want to go in case someone recognized him as a government agent. He doesn't really have a cover story here in San Francisco. He's thinking we need to be extra careful around anything concerning art. So, I guess we both go."

Chapter 35

IN ANOTHER PART of San Francisco, an additional wave of rage came over him. His headache had increased to epic proportions, his jaw ached from clenching and unclenching it, his fists hurt from pounding them on the marble table top, and his foot hurt from kicking the ottoman. Pain was taking over again.

"I'm dealing with incompetent idiots here. Total screw-ups. All of them. Why can't these big, burly men get rid of a small, helpless woman? What's so tough about that? Just blow up her damn car. Nothing sophisticated about that. It's a freaking bomb. It has to work."

He placed a phone call, and when George answered, he lit into him, not letting George get a word in. When he ran out of names to call him and nasty things he was going to do to him, he paused.

George spoke up. "But, Boss. It was rigged exactly like it should have been. I don't know what happened. Maybe that no good guy sold me a dud. That's gotta be it. A dud. Otherwise, it would have blown her into little pieces."

"I don't care. It didn't explode. She's still alive, right?"

"Yeah, she is. She's went for a drive, and I lost her somewhere near the wharf."

"What? You lost her? Again? You idiot. Any idea where she is now?"

"Yeah, I found her again. She went back home. She's still there. I been watchin' her house."

"Okay. You have one more time to make up for this shitty screw up. My primary target is a blonde woman. This first bomb was supposed to get rid of her friend and scare the bejesus out of the blonde. But, since you screwed up, and the first woman is still alive, you'll have to kill them both now. There's a party in two days, and I've already emailed you the address and a description of the blonde. Make sure you know what she looks like.

"Now, this is how I want it to go down. Get a bigger bomb. I'll send you a description of the blonde's car. This time, I want that bomb on that car to create a big mess. Sensational. Kaboom. No one lives this time. Got it? I want the blonde woman's death to be spectacular.

"Bottom line, I want them both dead. DEAD. Do I make myself clear? I won't tolerate anything less.

"And, don't even think of not following through. You do remember France, don't you? Only this time, it'll be you on the receiving end."

"Yeah. I got it. It'll get done, Boss." It was too late for his boss to hear him, as the call had already been disconnected. "Damn. I need to get a new device made soon. Okay. Time to get busy. I'm done watching her place. She ain't goin' nowhere."

Chapter 36

IN THE HILLS north of Venice, Serge woke up from another restless night. "Damn. Why do I keep having these dreams? I don't like it. All the more reason to be done with this dude and his forged paintings. It's still early. I'm going to make some breakfast and do some more research on Interpol agents. I'd really like to talk to someone about this mess. Harry's right. I'm glad I kept all the evidence."

He busied himself with breakfast and worked a while on his laptop computer, when he heard a vehicle pull into his driveway. Looking out the window, he didn't recognize the dark sedan with tinted windows. A chill went up his spine. He sent a quick text to Harry telling him he had a visitor he didn't know and was worried. Thinking he should hide his laptop, he decided he'd put it in the oven. "Not the best, but good enough for now. Whoever this is doesn't need to see it."

He kept watching the car. Eventually, one man, dressed from head to toe in black, stepped out and looked around. He made his way to the front door and knocked. Another chill came over Serge. He looked at his phone to see if Harry responded and sent him another quick text to let him know he should come as quickly as he could. Then, he tossed his phone in the freezer.

"Hello. May I help you?" Serge opened the door just a crack and smiled at the huge, muscular man. Serge, fairly tall at six-foot, two-inches, had to look up. The man didn't return his smile as he forced his way past Serge and into the living room. "May I help you?" Serge was more forceful, trying to stand his ground.

"I've come with a message from the Boss. You can't call the shots. He does. That's why he's the Boss. Got it?"

"Ah, sure. Whatever. Tell him he's right. Anything else?"

"See here, Mr. Funny Business. You don't get it, do you? You can't just quit. No one just quits the Boss. I'm here to remind you of that."

Serge had a feeling of déjà vu and ducked when he saw the guy pull his arm back. The guy missed Serge's head, but grabbed his arm and twisted it behind his back. Serge yelped in pain. "Let go. I told you I won't quit. It's all a mistake."

"Let's just make sure you know who you're dealing with. You need to be reminded. No more talk of quitting."

Serge took a deep breath and twisted free, then grabbed a vase, and threw it at the big guy. His aim was off, and he missed by a mile. The man smiled. "You're a nothing, and you need to be taught a lesson. You can't hurt me." He lunged at Serge, catching him by the shirtsleeve. Serge flipped around, kicked at the guy's face, catching him off guard. He scored a weak hit on his cheek. As the guy rubbed his cheek, Serge saw a book on the coffee table. He grabbed it and swung at his head. It connected with his ear, but didn't seem to slow him down. Another book went sailing past his head as Serge looked around for more things to use.

The big guy ducked and lunged once more at Serge, just as Serge grabbed a pen. His grip was off, and instead of jamming it in his eye or throat, he ended up making a small hole in the guy's jacket. The big guy looked down at his jacket as Serge tried to back up, still looking for anything else he could grab to use against him.

The little mark on the jacket seemed to make him madder, and he let go of Serge. "You weasel. I just bought this, and now you've ruined it." He grunted, let out a yell, and dived at Serge. Serge jumped to his left, but not before the guy grabbed his legs out from under him. Serge went down hard, hitting his head on the corner of the coffee table. Blood poured out of the back of his head as he lay there. He didn't move.

The guy stood over him, kicked him, and looked around. "Damn. I wasn't supposed to kill him. I'd better get the paintings the Boss wants and get out of here." Searching through the house and the art studio, he found nothing. "Where could they be? Did the courier already pick them up? Or, did this jerk hide them somewhere?" He searched again and decided he could waste no more time here.

"I could try to wipe my fingerprints off everything or I could just burn down the place. That makes more sense. He lit some paper on fire, scattered some more about to catch the flames, and ran out to his car. Throwing it into reverse, he spewed gravel and rocks as he sped away from Serge's slowly burning house.

Chapter 37

HARRY FELT THE phone in his pocket buzz a couple of times, but he was with a new client and didn't take time to look at it. Once he finished explaining his ideas and giving his estimate for a complete new garden and outdoor eating and entertaining area, he took out his phone. Seeing two texts from Serge, he read the first one.

"Yikes. That's not good." Then, he read the second and became more alarmed. "I need to get out there and see what's going on."

He left the estate where he had been meeting with his new client, sped through town, and headed up the hill to Serge's. As the road turned left into Serge's driveway, he noticed a little smoke coming from the house, and called the local fire department. He jumped out of his car, ran through the wide-open front door, and into the slightly smoky house. Covering his nose with his arm, he saw Serge lying on the floor and started to drag him toward the front door. That's when he noticed the red stain by his head.

"Serge. Serge, can you hear me?" No response.

He felt his neck for a pulse and thought he felt a weak one. Grabbing a towel from the kitchen, he tried to wrap it on Serge's head as he continued to pull him outside. "Serge, stay with me." He took a second to look at his head and noticed it didn't look good. As the fire department pulled up, he called to the first firefighter who jumped out of the truck. "I don't see a lot of fire, but he's hurt bad. We need an ambulance."

"One's on the way." The firefighter motioned to the vehicle pulling into the driveway. "We always call them, too."

The paramedics took over for Harry and whisked Serge away. Harry tried to ask what they thought, but they didn't answer him. He turned back to the firemen who had the wispy smoke under control. The first firefighter came over to Harry. "What can you tell us about this?"

Harry showed the two text messages to the firefighter. "That's all I know. I have no idea who he was or if he's the one who caused this."

"Well, he wasn't good at starting fires. He burned some magazines and newspapers. But, they caused more smoke damage than fire damage. He probably thought no one would be around for a while, and it would eventually burn the house."

"How soon do you think they'll know anything about Serge?"

"I wouldn't guess. The police are coming and my guys need to finish up here. I'm sure the police will want to know if you are familiar enough with him and his things to know if something is missing."

"He's my friend and I've been here a bunch and I know he has a laptop and a cell phone. The phone's probably in his pocket, though. Then, he has his artist supplies in his studio." Harry started walking through the house to the studio.

"Don't touch anything." The firefighter handed a pair of gloves to Harry. One police car pulled up and the officer talked to the head firefighter."

"Is it okay if I just look through the house? I might find his laptop."

"We need to process it first. Who are you?"

"I'm his friend, Harry. He texted me about someone who had come here today." Harry looked around. "This place is a mess and Serge was meticulous. He wouldn't live like this. Whoever was here must have been looking for something, but I really don't think he had any valuables lying around. Do you think it's a burglary gone bad?"

"We won't know until the investigation is complete. You said he had a laptop. We'll need that."

Searching the house and the studio, no laptop was found. Harry had stayed in the kitchen, sitting at the table, when the firefighter and police officer entered. "What was that? What was that noise?" Harry looked around.

The firefighter looked at Harry. "I didn't hear anything. What did it sound like?"

"A faint beep. Like when I get a message on my computer or my phone." They listened and heard nothing else.

"I must have imagined it. But, it really sounded like it came from over here." Harry walked toward the refrigerator. "Maybe he has an alarm on his freezer. Oh, hey the door isn't quite shut." He closed the door.

"Why don't you see what's in there? Maybe the fire starter put something in his freezer." The policeman motioned to the door.

Harry opened the freezer and the phone lying on a package of meat beeped again. "Well, I'll be. His phone is in the freezer. Why would he do that?"

"We'll need to take that downtown. Do you think you can access it?"

"Yeah, I'm pretty sure I can. We gave each other our passwords for our phones, computers, and alarms in case we needed to help each other out." Harry put on the gloves handed to him by the police officer, unlocked Serge's phone, and retrieved his last two messages. "He has two voicemail messages. Both are from a secure number." He put the phone on speaker and they all listened as the caller mentioned a reference to an inquiry Serge made. "Now, if we just had his laptop."

The firefighter walked to the oven. "I've seen stranger things. But, if you put your phone in the freezer, why not put your laptop in your oven?" He opened the oven and looked at Harry. "Jackpot."

Chapter 38

HARRY PULLED THE laptop out of the oven and looked at the firefighter and the policeman. "Why the hell would he put his phone in the freezer and his laptop in the oven?"

"Was it possible he knew whoever was here and didn't want him to see them?"

"I suppose, although his texts didn't really sound like he knew the guy. He just sounded like he was very concerned."

"Any idea what he would be concerned about?"

Harry took a deep breath, looked away, and then back at the two men. "Yeah, I do. He was involved in some pretty deep shit."

"Then it's time we all went to the police station." He nodded to Harry and the head firefighter, who had just been handed some items in a bag by one of his men.

"It wasn't an accident, based on the book of matches my guys just found."

Harry nodded as they left Serge's house.

Chapter 39

AT THE POLICE station, Harry, the firefighter, and policeman were led into a conference room by two detectives. First, the firefighter filled the police inspectors in on the fire, showed him the book of matches, and voiced his initial concerns. "We'll know more once our investigator finishes, and then we can give you a detailed report."

Harry had been listening to the firefighter and the questions the police detectives asked. When they looked at him and asked him to relate what he knew, he smiled, took a deep breath, and began. "I'll tell you what I know, and then I think I should look at Serge's laptop. I may be able to tell you if anything is there."

He started with what Serge had told him recently, showed them the texts Serge sent to him, had them listen to the voicemails on Serge's phone, and ended with Serge's desire to be finished forging paintings.

"Do you know who was paying him to forge these?" Both detectives were taking notes.

"No. And, I'm fairly certain Serge didn't either. He said initially the guy in the bar at college was a big guy, but he looked like a regular guy. I don't think he paid a lot of attention to him. He was focused on the money. And, here, he said a different courier came each time to pick up the paintings. Oh, I almost forgot. His last three paintings are in a crate in the back room of my shop."

"Why are they there?"

"After Serge got this last voicemail, I think he was really worried. He'd been beat up before, and I think he must have wanted some leverage or at least didn't want to make it easy for the courier to get them. So, he sent the crate home with me. I put it in my storeroom to keep for him. He said he would get it in a couple of days."

"We'll need those." Harry nodded.

One of the police detectives had left the room and returned with three sheets of paper. He showed them to the other detective, and they had a quiet conversation.

Harry looked at the firefighter. "Do you think the hospital will call you or me? I'd like to go there and see how Serge is doing. I really think I felt a pulse when I first got there."

The detectives had finished their conversation and turned to Harry. "We have a bigger problem than your friend realized. This is a bulletin from Interpol about a forgery ring that encompasses Italy, especially this area and Venice, and France. It may stretch to the United States. There have been some forgeries discovered that may point to the actual forger. Something about a key. We need to go with you to the hospital. I hope your friend can talk."

At the mention of a key and Interpol, Harry looked up. "Wait a minute. Serge was looking into becoming an Interpol agent. Let me think. And, he mentioned painting a key. Damn. Why didn't I pay more attention to what he said?"

"Tell me again what you know about a key. That may be important, especially reading this bulletin."

"Well, Detective, I believe he truly thought he was in danger. But, he also was worried that whoever is paying him to paint the forgeries would turn him in, and nobody would believe him. I know he wanted to be done with this mess but wasn't sure how to get out. I remember him telling me that a high-end lab or expert would find some key. That's about all I remember. Sorry."

"That's okay. It's more than we had, and I'll pass that info on to Interpol. Now, let's all go to the hospital. We need to talk to him. Then, we need to run those calls on his phone. I'm not optimistic we'll find out where they're from, but we have to try."

Chapter 40

THINGS WERE NOT going as planned. At all.

When Carlo left Serge's place, he headed straight toward his safe house outside of Venice. He had no intention of calling his boss nor going to his boss's apartment in Venice. Serge was dead, and his boss told him specifically to rough him up, not kill him. Carlo had no paintings, and his boss specifically told him to pick up the paintings.

He'd have to think about this for a while. His boss didn't tolerate mistakes. He had been a witness to what happened to those who messed up, and it wasn't pleasant. The lucky ones were killed outright. There was no way he was going to end up like any of those. And, he certainly wasn't going to get caught in the middle, between his boss and Dixie. No way. That chick was scary.

He was sure his boss would be calling him, and he needed to figure out what to tell him. Mumbling to no one in particular as he drove, he started to form a plan. "I could tell him the house was on fire when I got there, and I couldn't go in. He'd never know that it wasn't. That way he'd think the paintings burned up and Serge with them. He'd have to believe me." He shook his head. "Probably not. And, definitely not her."

Driving further, he looked out the window, not seeing the lush, green countryside. "Or, I could just disappear. I can grab a different identity and start over. After all, I kept the money from selling the painting to that broad in San Francisco. I'll just start a new life. Somewhere he can't find me." He smiled to himself. "I think that's the best plan. I don't need him anymore."

Satisfied, he drove on. His ringing phone startled him, and he didn't' answer it. After a couple of minutes, he listened to the voicemail. "Carlo, you imbecile. Why haven't I heard from you. You'd better not have screwed up this assignment. I need those paintings, and I need them ASAP. Where the hell are you? Remember what happens to those who can't follow my instructions? Now, call me. If I don't hear from you in an hour, you'll wish you were dead. Got it?"

After he stopped the car and listened to the message, he threw the phone toward the field. "Damn. He is such a bloody tyrant. I'm going to get a new phone. That way he won't be able to find me. Ever.

"I'm outta here."

Chapter 41

IN SAN FRANCISCO, Marta took a call from Clark. "I've missed talking to you. How are you doing?" After a few minutes, the conversation then turned professional. "Is the same car still following you? Have you been able to find out any more about it?"

"I'm keeping close tabs on my surroundings, Clark. I keep seeing that blue car, but I can never see the driver or see if anyone else is in the car, because the windows are so dark. And, there are no license plates."

"Have you learned anything more about the paintings?"

"Some, and what we uncovered here may pertain to you or Suzie. Both of you can keep an eye out for paintings that might match what we've found. Everything points to three main places, well actually four. We have the two issues in Paris, the issues in southern France, in Venice, and in San Francisco. Pete is working in Venice on some things and will be calling you later. Are you still going to that art patron's birthday party, or whatever it is?"

"Yeah. Funny thing about that. I received an invitation, too, but it was addressed incorrectly. Neither Suzie nor I know him. But, we thought we'd go together. For now, Suzie is staying here, and Agent Greg Mitchell is here as well. I've put you on speaker."

"Hi, everyone. Stay extra careful and watchful, Marta. Both you and Suzie need to watch what you're doing and who is around you, especially at this party."

"We will." Marta continued to fill Clark in on the day's events as Suzie and Greg added their comments.

"So, Clark, can you tell us what's going on in France, and what paintings we need to look for?"

"Greg, this is what we have and what we know. We're still searching for the why and the ultimate who, although we're getting closer. Here goes: So many things point to Sir Anthony Furst, a billionaire from London. He's wanted for questioning by several agencies in a wide range of art related activities. We all agree he's involved somehow in most of the activities, including the murders. The thing is, no one knows for sure what he looks like, as he's quite the recluse. And, we're sure he has a team working for him.

"As for the auction houses, we are fairly certain we have a handle on the individuals who have sold or bought forgeries in the last year or so. The list has dwindled considerably."

"That's good, right?"

"Yes and no, Marta. Yes, in that we have two recent shipments of paintings that have some odd paper and some type of dried grass in their packing crates. These are our first real clues of where the forgeries might be originating. Our lab experts have discovered an odd symbol under one layer of paint. I should know more about that fairly soon.

"As for the list of buyers and sellers, it's a big question mark and a huge concern. Most of the previous people who had any type of contact with those stolen and forged paintings are dead. We're keeping these two new shipments under wraps and protecting the people who bought them. We still aren't sure if they were duped or if they had anything to do with the forgeries." Clark didn't elaborate on the murders, as he didn't want to upset Suzie.

"So, what do you want us to do, Clark?"

"For starters, Marta, I've emailed you a detailed list of the paintings we feel are still missing. These would be originals. A couple are from museums; three or four are from private galleries, and at least two are from private collectors. All had been authenticated;

all had provenances, and all were replaced with forgeries. Damn good forgeries, however."

"Do you really think my shop will see any of these?"

"Suzie, who knows? The thing is, you've already been contacted with the forged Monet. Maybe that's something; maybe not. And, Marta was attacked for asking questions. These threads are important. We just don't know how, yet."

"If the forgeries were that good, how did anyone find out they were actually forgeries?"

"Good question, Greg. One of the museums was updating its records and insurance, and an appraiser caught it. Apparently, last year they had some disturbance that caused their security to go down. Private security was called in, and they figured the swap took place at that time. They put out notices to other museums and discovered that another museum had exactly the same thing happen. They lost a painting as well.

"Our lab is positive they both were painted by the same person. Then, there are galleries and collectors in Italy and in France with forgeries. Again, they thought they had originals."

"How can you be certain you have all of the forgeries located?"

"Well, Marta, we can't be absolutely sure. The world of collection and gallery pieces is pretty tight. They talk to one another, sort of. It's possible there are others out there, and those people just don't want to go public yet. That's what makes it so hard. The list I sent to you is of the ones we're definitely looking for, though.

"Now, I need to fill you in on Pete."

$\mathcal{C}$hapter 42

"WHAT ABOUT PETE?"

"A small shop in Venice, owned by two men, received a crate with a painting they didn't order. About a week prior to that, one of the owners had been notified about his brother being killed in the south of France. His brother was one of those gallery owners who had a forged painting. Now, fast forward to this delivery, and needless to say, the owners both became worried and contacted Interpol.

"Pete picked up the crate with the painting and took it to our lab in Venice, where they identified the packing paper used in that crate. It had some business names listed on it from a town somewhere north of Venice, and he's headed to that town as we speak.

"The gallery owners are cooperating, and we've not involved anyone else. So far, it's all under wraps so as not to cause alarm. The painting, however, is a forgery. Again, a great piece of work, but it has that same symbol, and our guys are working to figure out what it might mean. And, get this. The original hangs in a museum in Venice.

"But, here's a side note, Marta. This gallery is right next door to the one where you saw the workman hang or remove that small Manet. Before you were attacked. Things are just a little too close for me."

"What? I don't get it, Clark. None of it."

"I know. First, it's too coincidental. Why send a forgery to a small shop who didn't order it? Unless, it was delivered by mistake or the address was incorrect. It's possible that it was to have been delivered to the gallery where you were, Marta. But, why send a forgery of a painting everybody already knows hangs in a prestigious gallery? Why use packing paper that might lead you to a clue?

"But, there's more. Did I mention the shop is owned by two men? The first one, like I said, was related to one of our dead owners in France. Well, it turns out the other one came from the town listed on the packing material. He's been gone from there for several years, but he recognized the business names right away. What connection this is, we don't know yet. We'll know more when Pete gets there and looks around. The forger may live there. Or, the whole operation could be centered there.

"We'll keep you posted on him. In the meantime, just pay attention to the list I emailed to you. Suzie, if anyone else wants to sell a painting to you, let one of the agents know right away. And, pay attention to anyone coming in your shop that you don't recognize. I know you have new clients all the time, but be especially aware for the next few weeks.

"Marta, I want you to go over the list of people who signed up for your upcoming tours. I mean, run background checks if you have to. Did anyone seem like they're overly interested in any of the paintings, especially those on the list? Did anyone seem out of place for an art tour? Do you meet with them as a group in the next week or so, or do you meet with them individually?"

"I meet with them as a group and have already had two meetings, Clark. We have our final meeting two days from now. I guess I could meet individually this time. Maybe somebody would raise a red flag."

"Why don't you keep your group meeting, and then meet with them individually, too, Marta. I'd like one of the agents to be there as well. Agent Mitchell, can you put someone on this and have them pose as one of the people on the tour? Now, have fun at the party, but keep your eyes and ears open."

Chapter 43

LATER, MARTA AND Suzie were getting ready to go to the birthday party. Agent Mitchell was waiting in the kitchen, talking to both Shadow and Lady. He stood up when they entered the kitchen. Both in short, elegant, black cocktail dresses, sky-high heels, Marta's blonde hair curled, and Suzie's dark hair piled on top of her head. Greg stared as they walked toward him.

Finally, he found his voice. "Wow! You both look fantastic. Wish I could go with you."

"Thanks. We decided we should look the part to attend a posh party."

"I'd say you accomplished that. And more. I almost forgot the plan," he said with a grin before continuing. "Okay, here goes. I'll drive you and drop you off about a block or so away. That way we can all see what's going on or if you're being followed on foot. We'll have another car tailing us until we get close. Now, when you're ready to leave the party, just text me. I'll be there in less than three minutes. If anyone asks or gets suspicious, tell them your driver is picking you up. Okay?

"You both have the signal devices in your purses, right? In case your purses are inspected, these look just like lipstick. Just hit the button at the bottom of the tube like I showed you, if anything appears really strange or someone tries something funny.

"As we talked, be very interested, but not suspiciously so, in the paintings in this place. Discuss them or whatever so it doesn't look odd to anyone. You know what you're doing there. You have the list from Clark memorized?"

"Yes, we both know what's on that list, Greg."

"Good, Marta. I figured. Remember I told you we had an agent working for the catering company and that he would be in the kitchen?"

"What do you mean 'had'?"

"Well, that company has been replaced by another one. Interesting, to say the least. We couldn't even get to the new company without revealing who we are. That means you have no one on the inside. You will, however, have several agents close by. Just, be careful.

"You still want to go through with this, ladies?"

"Absolutely. I want to know if this is all tied to someone trying to kill me. Twice."

"And, I want to know about my attacker."

"I understand. Please be careful, both of you. Okay?"

"I'd feel better if I wasn't wearing these heels. It's kind of hard to kick someone when I'm teetering on four inch heels."

"Marta, they look fantastic, but I have no idea how you even walk in those, let alone anything else. You'll do fine. Ready, ladies?"

"Let's go."

Chapter 44

GREG LET MARTA and Suzie out about a block away, and they made their way toward the festively lit mansion in the Sea Cliff area. Limos were taking turns pulling up to the grand entrance, depositing their elegantly dressed occupants to the attentive doormen. Marta and Suzie waited to cross the street as a dark red Mercedes pulled into a just-vacated parking spot on the corner in front of them.

"Hey, that car looks just like mine." Marta stopped and gestured to the dark, maroon sports car.

A slightly older woman with blonde hair stepped out, smoothed her black cocktail dress, put her hands on her hips, and mumbled. "Damn seat. I still can't get it right."

Marta and Suzie were right by the car and couldn't help but hear. "I'm sorry. I didn't mean to eavesdrop, but are you having problems with the seat?"

The woman looked at Marta. "Yes, I am. I just bought this car two weeks ago, and the salesman told me how to get the seat to fit me, but for the life of me, I can't get it right. I'm short, and I have to keep messing with it every time I drive it. I thought it was a smart seat."

"It can be tricky at first. But, once you set it, it remembers you by the key you use. Are you the only one who drives it?"

"I am. Do you know how to set it?"

"I do. I have this exact same car, same color and everything. Here, let me first clear it, and then you can set it. I'll help you." The woman motioned for Marta to get in and set the controls. Then Marta had the woman sit in and the seat adjusted. "Now, watch what happens when I reset the seat for someone taller." Marta moved the seat, got out, and locked the car. She then unlocked it with the woman's key and the seat moved.

"Well, I'll be. You just solved my problem. I'll buy you a drink. Are you going to this gaudy, overdone, so-called birthday bash?"

"Glad I could help. And, yes, we are." Marta introduced Suzie and herself to the woman, mentioning that Suzie was in the art business and that she was in the travel business. "How about you? Are you going to the same party?"

"Yes, I am. I'm Maxine Small, by the way. I used to collect art, but now I have too much. I need to visit with you, Suzie, about disposing of some of it. You might know another collector who would appreciate having a chance to have some of my pieces. We'll talk. Do you know the host, Thomas Smith?"

"No. Neither of us knows him nor his aunt. We figured we were invited due to our businesses. Why?"

"He's a pompous jackass. Pardon me. But, he is. All show, throws his money around, and thinks he knows art. He doesn't. I don't even know why he tells people he's a patron of the art scene. I think he dribbles some money their way once in a while. You'll see when you meet him. And, he likes to dress like he's important. Oh, I should have let you form your own opinions."

Maxine smiled. "For that matter, I really don't think he has an aunt. Who knows if he even has a mother. Probably an alien for all I know. And, this outrageous shindig? It's just an excuse to show off his newest acquisitions. Did I mention he's a pompous jackass?"

Marta had closed Maxine's car door and handed the keys to her as she chuckled at Maxine's description. As they talked, they crossed the street and were welcomed by a doorman on the curb. He smiled and directed them toward the front door.

"Okay. I'll be quiet now. Once you girls meet our esteemed host, come find me. Then, you can give me your opinions. I'll bet you both agree with me."

Maxine smiled at the doorman and led the way up the massive stone steps, which were flanked on either side by elaborate, Grecian statues, gilded planters spilling their colorful, blooming flowers, bubbling, marble fountains, and dozens of lights. More gaudy statues and gold pots covered the top step, all vying for attention. The equally massive, carved, wooden front door sat opened wide, revealing a grand foyer large enough to serve as its own apartment. Above it all, the enormous, crystal chandelier sent dancing sparkles to every square inch of the room and beyond. Polished to a high sheen, the parquet floor, with its intricate center medallion, looked like it belonged in its own museum. Marta and Suzie followed Maxine, as Suzie turned, wide-eyed, to Marta. Marta nodded. "Quite impressive."

"Overdone, if you ask me. Guess he's trying to prove he has more money than taste." Maxine mumbled over her shoulder to Marta, making her chuckle once again at this delightful woman.

Standing just inside the spacious foyer was an elegantly dressed man, who could easily pass for a tuxedo model. The smile plastered on his face showed a perfect smile, but no warmth. Close behind him was a slim woman, equally as elegant in her soft gray sheath. Her steely stare, as she scanned the people coming through the doorway, briefly flicked over the three ladies. Marta smiled at her. She looked right through Marta.

"Welcome to our little party, ladies. I don't believe I've had the pleasure of meeting you before." His honey-sweet voice almost dripped from his mouth as he grabbed Maxine's hand and held it several seconds too long. He repeated the greeting with Suzie and then Marta. Marta looked at his eyes. What she noticed chilled her to the bone. It was if there was no life behind those dark eyes. She shuddered. He put his hand on her shoulder. "My dear, are you cold? Dixie, get a wrap for our guest." He motioned to the slim woman behind him.

"No. I'm alright. Really. Don't bother." Marta smiled again to the woman, who hadn't moved. "Do I know you? You look awfully familiar."

The woman's eyes narrowed ever so slightly as her gaze bore a hole through the air. Thomas intervened. "I'm sure Dixie only looks like someone you know. She's a special friend." Her icy glare, dripping with frost, turned toward him.

"Again, welcome to our little gathering. I must see to other guests. Enjoy yourselves." Dismissing the three women, he turned to the next set of guests coming through the door, his smile never changing and his eyes never gaining any life.

Maxine practically snorted as they moved inside to the spacious, gaudy, grand salon with its dark red and gold walls. Paintings hung throughout the room, all slightly lit, with heavy gold ropes keeping people from getting too close. It was overly clear they weren't to be inspected at close range. "He acted like he's never met me before. Not that I care. But, what a jerk. I'll show him."

Marta nodded. "Did you look at his eyes? They're dead eyes. Like no life at all in him. He's spooky. But, his voice. It's so distinctive and too sweet. Almost syrupy. And, that woman. I know I've seen her before. I know it."

"You're right about his eyes, Marta. And, did you notice his smile? I've always thought he had too many facelifts or surgeries. Did you happen to see the veins on his forehead? Ready to pop, if you ask me. And, that woman looked like she wanted to smack you, Marta. Strange pair. Well, you girls go mingle. I'll catch up with you later. I need some dirt for my next column." With that remark, Maxine made her way to a well-dressed couple admiring a Monet.

Chapter 45

"SHE'S QUITE THE woman, Marta. I like her. But, I wonder what she means by gathering dirt for her column."

"I think I recognize her name. Isn't she a columnist for the Chronicle or the Examiner? Maybe she's looking for gossip for her column. I don't know. Tell you one thing, she's right on about the pair at the doorway. Strange doesn't even begin to describe them. Let's get a glass of champagne and look around." Marta glanced over her shoulder as they made their way toward a waiter with a tray of champagne. "I'm positive I've seen that woman before."

"What woman? The one by Thomas?"

"Yes, that one. She has such a distinctive look about her, but I can't think where I might have run into her. She's not the most pleasant person to have greeting people. Maybe she's his girlfriend or wife, however. Let's look at all his paintings and listen to gossip."

For the next two hours they wandered throughout the mansion, examined paintings, pretended to be interested when someone was near, watched Maxine work a room, listened in on conversations, and smiled or nodded to others. A couple of times Maxine caught up to them with a piece of information she was absolutely giddy about.

"Okay, here's the scoop on the stone-faced woman by the side of Thomas. One of my sources says she's actually a model from

Italy and poses nude for him as he paints her. Apparently, it doesn't take personality to pose. But, another one told me she runs this show, and Thomas is her minion. Who knows? I'll find out more and catch up with you." She chuckled and glided off to talk to someone she just recognized.

"She's a hoot. I like her. Maybe I'll get to know her better if she really does come to my shop with some paintings she'd like to sell."

They made their way into several more rooms, including the oversized ballroom off the grand salon. Each room was more ornate than the last, as if the rooms themselves were trying to outdo each other with their poor style. All had paintings. "This is beyond impressive. Who has this many pieces in their homes? Do you think they're all genuine? I mean, look at this Renoir. If I'm not mistaken, doesn't it hang in the Louvre? What's going on? By the way, I've seen at least a couple that are on the list you received from Clark. How about you?"

"I completely agree. That Renoir does hang in the Louvre. It's not a crime to have a replica, but he seems to treat these as originals. Don't these people know these aren't originals, or do they even care? And, in answer, yes. At least four are on that list from Clark. We can't get close enough to verify anything, and we might not be able to tell anyway. But, it is beginning to give me the chills. Let's try to find Maxine."

As they were making their way through the last small salon, Maxine came to where they were. "Well, girls, time for this old gal to head home. I have fodder for the column, and I want to blow this joint. I've had enough of stuffiness and fake smiles for one night. I'd really like to have coffee or wine with the two of you. You're both so nice and normal." She chuckled. "It's been great meeting you. And, thanks for fixing my seat. I just love that car, but the seat thing was driving me nuts."

"No problem. Glad I could help. And, yes, let's get together. You have my card, and I have yours. Maybe some morning this week for coffee would be good." Marta smiled at her as they walked. "We're finished here, too. My feet are killing me, and I'm tired of this place." Suzie stopped to talk to another couple. "Suzie is just saying goodbye to some clients of hers, and then we're out of here. Have a great night. I'll be in touch soon."

Maxine waved and headed out the door. Suzie caught up with Marta, who was watching Thomas walk out of the foyer with a large man and through a door along the far wall. The supposed model was glaring at their retreating backs, her arms folded across her chest and her frown evident. "He really does give me the creeps, especially his eyes. I don't care if I ever see him again. And, I'm certain I've seen the woman before. Geez, maybe I'm in the twilight zone."

Suzie laughed and nodded to the pair leaving the foyer. "That guy he's walking with is big enough to be a bodyguard."

"Right. In fact, he reminds me of a bodyguard at an art gallery in Venice. But, then again, all bodyguards probably look alike." Marta shrugged. "I just called for our ride, and he will be here in about three minutes. Let's head out. I'd rather wait outside than in here. Is that okay?"

As they headed out of the small salon, through the foyer, and toward the doorway, a large explosion cut through the night, followed by an orange fireball that lit up the night street in front of the mansion, sending shock waves and pieces of light in all directions.

People screamed. Marta was one of them.

Chapter 46

FROM INSIDE, PEOPLE rushed toward the mansion's front door, staring in horror at the burning mess just down the block. One blackened car frame sat in the middle of the street, destroyed beyond recognition, and two others were barely more than charred frames. Pieces of burning and smoldering metal lay in the street. Acrid smoke filled the air. Sirens could be heard in the distance.

Marta and Suzie stared from the top step. When her purse started buzzing, Marta was confused. As more people emerged from the mansion, they were forced to head down the steps toward the street. Once at street level, someone came up behind Marta and took her arm. "Let's go. The car is this way." Greg steered them down a side street into the waiting car. Once he had them both inside, he directed the driver. "Get us out of here. Fast. Head to the alternate route."

Marta gained her composure first. "What just happened?"

"Someone placed a bomb on a car. It went off when the car moved away from the curb."

"Was anyone in the car? Sorry. Stupid question. They had to be in order for it to be moved. Do you know who the car belonged to?" Marta was trying to look behind them as they sped away. Suzie sat still, in shock. Fire trucks and police cars were converging on the scene from every direction, lights flashing, sirens blaring. The driver headed away from the scene and toward the Golden Gate Bridge. "Where are we going?"

"We're going to cross the Golden Gate and pull into the Vista Point at the other side of the bridge. I want to make sure we're not being followed. Then, we'll head to your house, Marta."

"Why would we be followed? Did you see something?"

Agent Mitchell looked at the driver, who had been watching the rear view mirror. They crossed the bridge, pulled into the Vista parking lot, he jumped out, and made a phone call. Marta and Suzie looked at each other. When he got back in, he nodded to the driver. "We're clear. Let's get you both home. Then we can talk."

Marta had been thinking about what they saw from just inside the house and then as they stepped onto the front step. Things were coming back to her, slowly at first. All of a sudden, it hit her. "Oh my God. Was that Maxine's car? Was Maxine in that car, or had she already left? Agent Mitchell, we have to go back to see if she's okay." Even as she said it, she knew no one in or near that car would be okay.

"Marta, let's wait until we get to your house to talk about this. Okay? Hang on for a few more minutes." Traffic was light when they left Vista Point, turned around at the next exit, and headed back to The City.

Suzie was looking at Marta. "What happened? What's going on?" Coming out of shock, her hands were shaking as she folded and unfolded them in her lap.

Chapter 47

IN ITALY, HARRY and the two detectives arrived at the hospital, where they were met by the head surgeon. After understanding who they were, he looked at Harry. "It doesn't look good for your friend. He took a serious blow to his head and lost a lot of blood. To be perfectly honest, we're all surprised he made it this far. Right now, he's in a medically induced coma, and I don't look to change that for several days. I'm not allowing anyone in to see him for at least 24 hours."

He looked at the detectives. "And, certainly no one can talk to him for at least the next week."

The three looked at each other and then at the surgeon. "Did he say anything? I thought I felt a pulse when I dragged him out of his house."

"He did have a very weak pulse. But, he did not say anything. I'd suggest you come back tomorrow when you can have two minutes to sit with him. Does he have a next of kin?"

"The only one I know about is his uncle, and I will try to remember where he lives. I think his grandfather is dead, and I know his parents are dead. We have access to his laptop. Maybe there is something on it."

The detectives thanked the physician, and all three left the hospital. On the way back to the police station to pick up Harry's car, he asked the detectives if he could have Serge's laptop to search for family.

"We need to have it checked first. If our IT guy is at the station, we'll have him download a copy of everything on it, and then you can take it. Don't destroy or delete anything."

"I won't. I just want to find out more about his family. He didn't talk about them very much."

After all the data was copied and downloaded, the laptop was given to Harry. They agreed to meet in the morning at the hospital, and they told Harry to be careful. "If the person who did this to Serge is still looking for something he had, he may come back. Don't go to Serge's house. Got it?" Harry nodded and headed home with his friend's laptop and phone.

Over the next few hours, Harry combed through Serge's emails, bookmarked websites, and then his phone texts. Serge was neat and orderly, but Harry found very little of interest regarding the forgeries. He read two messages from someone telling him a courier was coming the next day. He hoped the IT guy at the police station could figure out where that email came from. As for relatives, there was only one email. And, that was informing Serge of a death in the family. It was from an attorney in Venice. He'd contact him in the morning to see if he knew of any other relatives.

He also decided to wait until morning to contact the number Interpol had left on Serge's phone.

$\mathcal{C}$hapter 48

IN THE MORNING Harry placed a call to Serge's attorney in Venice. After explaining to a secretary who he was, he was put through to an Italian Solicitor by the name of Gino Mazano. Once again he explained what had happened, telling Mr. Mazano he didn't know if Serge was alive or not.

"Harry, I will call the hospital. If my client is alive, all I can tell you is that he had a will. I will need to wait until I can talk to him."

"I understand, Mr. Mazano. Is there anything you can tell me about a next of kin? I'd like to call them and let them know. That is, if there is anyone I should call."

"My client listed a woman by the name of Francesca Ware as the contact person at his family's winery. There are no other living relatives. The winery and its circumstances are addressed in my client's will. I will make a call to the hospital and then contact you. Is there anything else?"

"No. Thank you. I am going to the hospital now. I'll talk to you later."

Harry hung up and headed to the hospital. Pulling up at the same time as the two police detectives, he told them about his conversation with Serge's attorney. As they entered the intensive care area, they were met by the chief surgeon.

Looking at Harry, he put his hand on his arm. "I'm so sorry to tell you this. Your friend did not survive the night. His wound was too grave, and he had lost too much blood. If it's any consolation, I believe he felt nothing after his head hit the floor."

Harry stared at the surgeon, who helped him sit. "Put your head down. I know this is a shock." The surgeon looked at the detectives, who sat down by Harry.

"Doctor, this is now a murder investigation. We will need your Medical Examiner's report and anything else you can tell us." One of the detectives touched Harry on the arm. Harry, tears streaming down his face, looked up.

"Serge would have never hurt anybody. Why did this happen? What do we do with those damn paintings? Can you catch whoever did this? What can I do? Why Serge? He was a good man." Harry sniffed into the tissue the surgeon handed to him. "What happens next?"

"We will gather all the information and evidence we can to start the investigation. You mentioned you have some of his paintings. We will need those as well. And, we'll need to visit with you some more to fill in any blanks we might have."

Harry nodded. "Where do we start?" The tears had stopped, but he still held onto the chair.

"First, we talk to his attorney. Then, you let us do our investigation. We will let you know what's going on and when we need to talk to you."

The surgeon stood up. "I'll notify Serge's attorney and send him a death certificate. Our M.E. will do an autopsy and send you the report." He looked at the detectives and then at Harry. "Harry, I know it's early. But, you need to think about burial. We have a counselor here at the hospital who can help you."

"Okay. I have no idea and so much to think about."

"Let's take one step at a time. I'll call the attorney, and then you and the detectives can talk to him. Okay?"

Chapter 49

HARRY COMPOSED HIMSELF and headed home to call Serge's attorney. By the time he called, the hospital had already sent a preliminary copy of the death certificate.

"For a formal reading of my client's will, I will make an appointment in your town, with my colleague who Serge was working with. That way, you won't have to come to Venice. But, for now, here are the main points.

"You will want to visit with Francesca Ware at my client's family vineyard and winery. She has some information for you. Serge instructed her to give you the information in case anything happened to him."

"May I interrupt?"

"Of course. What do you need?"

"When did Serge make his will?"

"He first came to our firm about three years ago, when his grandfather passed away. Then, one month ago he updated everything in his will. Why?"

"I'm just curious. I wondered if he knew something was going to happen."

"What do you mean?"

"Well, the police are investigating this as a murder now. They will want to talk to you, in case there is anything you can tell them."

"Okay. Please be sure to tell Ms. Ware that. It may be of significance to her operation."

"I will. Sorry to get off track. Please proceed."

"As I mentioned, you will want to visit with a Ms. Francesca Ware. I suggest doing that as soon as you can. It would be good to make an appointment and go visit her. There are some things she has for you and some issues to discuss with you.

"Next, I need you to know Serge left everything else to you: his home, his studio, all his furnishings, and a considerable savings account. You will need to meet with my colleague to sign the papers, provide identification, etc."

Harry was silent as he tried to process what Mr. Mazano had just said.

"Sir, are you still there?"

"Yeah. I'm just wondering some things. Why leave it all to me? I guess it was because he didn't have any relatives. But, the money? Why me? What am I going to do with any of his things?"

"I can only tell you my client was adamant about leaving everything to you. We don't know the reasons why. Are you okay? Perhaps you just need some time for it all to sink in. Can you go to our solicitor's office tomorrow? We like to wrap things up as soon as we can."

"Yeah, I can get there. Oh. I almost forgot. Did Serge mention burial?" Harry's eyes misted over when he thought about burying his best friend.

"Yes. He did. He has all the arrangements made, and you will be getting a call from the funeral home. He wished to be cremated and his ashes scattered in his grandfather's vineyards. That's another issue you need to visit with Ms. Ware about. The funeral home will contact the hospital and take care of those arrangements. They will notify you when that is to happen. Do you have any other questions for now?"

"No. Thank you."

"My colleague will call you, and please contact Ms. Ware as soon as you can. I will be in touch in a couple of days."

Harry hung up just as another call came through.

Chapter 50

ONE OF THE detectives was calling, asking him to come to the police station. They had more questions and some information for him. Harry told them he'd be there as soon as he made a couple of calls.

Placing a call to Francesca Ware, he left a message. "Ms. Ware, my name is Harry, and I'm a friend of Serge. I need to visit with you about some issues regarding Serge." He left that short message and his number. Mumbling to himself, he shook his head. "I don't know if she's been told about Serge. For all I know, she's 102 years old. I don't want to give her a heart attack or anything. What a mess."

His second call went to the attorney in town, where they set an appointment for tomorrow. Then, he headed to the police station, taking the crate of Serge's paintings with him.

Once there he met with the same detectives and the IT person. He filled them in on his call with Serge's attorney and told them about the meeting tomorrow. "I guess Serge's house and studio are now mine. I'm not sure what to do about that for now. This is the crate Serge asked me to keep for a few days. I haven't opened it, but I assume it has the last three paintings he did."

The detectives put on gloves and opened the crate. Inside were three museum-quality paintings, rolls of packing paper, and some dried grass. "Do these look familiar?" One detective motioned to Harry.

"Well, yes. In a couple of ways. I've seen Serge working on this one, before it was finished. And, this other one reminds me of a famous one I've seen somewhere. Are these forgeries?"

"Interpol thinks they are. Do you think Serge actually painted these?"

"Yeah, I'd bet on it. Why?"

"Well, that's our question. Why? Let's start from the beginning about what you know about his paintings and who he was painting for."

Harry again told them everything he knew, from Serge's latest revelations and explanations from a couple days ago to what he had seen Serge paint in the last few years. "I believe he was painting more and more just recently. It always seemed like he had one or two things he was working on. When I first met him, I thought he was just painting landscapes and selling them. When I started looking more closely, I realized he was painting copies of things which had already been done. You know, Monet, Renoir, and those artists. Painting their exact works."

"Forgeries?"

"Yeah, I guess. In fact, I asked him about this a couple of times, and he said he knew he was painting copies of important works. At first, he thought someone wanted a nice, well painted copy because they couldn't afford the original or the original was hanging in a museum somewhere. He really didn't think they were going to be passed off as originals. It wasn't until recently that I think he really began to wonder if they were being sold as the real deal. Then, about five or six months ago he really became suspicious. I'm sure he said that's when he started painting some sort of clue on the paintings.

"He also told me he was beat up a couple of times, when he told someone he wanted to quit. That's why I think he texted me the day he died. He was scared."

"Do you have any idea who was paying him? Did he ever say a name?"

"No. That's just it. He said he had one phone number where he could leave a text message. But, whoever was paying him always called him from a private number. When he tried to call that number, he got nothing. And, apparently, the courier who came to pick up the paintings was different each time."

"Do you know how he got paid?"

"He said money would appear in the mail."

"You mean, actually mail cash to him?"

"That's what he said. Sometimes it would be in his mailbox, but not actually mailed. It was like someone put it there."

"Okay. Thanks. We've been tracing his emails and so far, no consistent luck. One came from London and one from San Francisco. We've just involved Interpol. Let us know what you find at the winery."

Harry left and was just about home when his phone rang. It was Francesca Ware, and she didn't sound like he had pictured her; she sounded younger than he imagined. After a brief conversation, Harry set a time to visit her tomorrow after his visit with the attorney.

Chapter 51

WHILE HARRY WAS talking to Francesca in Italy, Agents Mitchell and Hansen had taken Marta and Suzie to Marta's home in San Francisco, where Lady and Shadow greeted them at the kitchen door. Normally, Shadow purred and begged to be picked up when Marta came home. This time, he wouldn't let her put him down. "What's going on, Shadow? Do you sense something?"

Both agents made some phone calls while Suzie sat, hugging Lady, staring into space. Greg knelt down to face her. "Are you up to talking about the night's events? We have not been followed and are safe here. There will be more security in about an hour, and we'll call Clark and Ian once we all put the pieces together." Suzie nodded.

He looked at Marta. "Can you tell us about the evening?"

Marta had opened some wine and even the agents had a glass in front of them. She sighed. "First, I'll tell you what I remember, and then I have questions. Dozens of questions. Okay?"

"Certainly."

Marta told the agents what she remembered, starting with meeting Maxine Small at her car, and ending with seeing the fireball and hearing the explosion from just inside the front door. She focused on details about the party, their host, the woman by his side, the bodyguard, and the paintings.

"I know several people said she was a model, but she reminds me of a woman I saw in Venice. It's coming back to me now. I'm positive she was Simone from a gallery or shop I was in. Positive. And, that bodyguard? He was in Venice, too. I'd bet money on it.

"Like I said, Thomas Smith has the deadest, creepiest eyes I've ever seen.

"And, some of the paintings we were looking for are hanging in his salons. They were roped off so people couldn't get within about four feet of them. I mean, seriously roped off. The lighting wasn't the best either, probably by design. They could be real; they could be forgeries that look really good, or they could be replicas by design. But, of the list Ian and Clark sent, there were at least four by my count. Suzie may have noticed more. We tried to split up some. That house is so damned huge." Marta looked at Suzie, who seemed to be coming out of her shocked state.

"Good work, Marta. Those descriptions have been sent to Ian and Clark. The people and the paintings."

"Okay. Now for my questions."

"Just a minute. Suzie, can you add anything to what Marta just said?" He spoke softly to Suzie as he petted Lady. "Are you doing okay? Can I get you anything?"

Suzie looked up at him. The shock and fear were almost gone from her face, and she smiled. "I'm okay. My brain is beginning to absorb what happened. I think. And, I agree with what Marta said. There might have been another painting you didn't see, Marta. I was in a smaller salon speaking with some clients of mine, and we remarked about a Monet he had hanging there. It took up one whole wall, but we couldn't get close to it at all. We remarked that it looked so real, but that we had all seen the original in Paris. I remember thinking it was a good fake. That was right before we got ready to leave. So, what happened?"

Agent Mitchell's phone rang, and he stepped into the foyer to take the call. When he came back, he looked at Marta and Suzie. "Ladies, can you handle some bad news?"

Chapter 52

MARTA NODDED, AND Suzie held onto Lady.

Taking a deep breath, he decided to give them the facts, as they knew them. "There was indeed a bomb-like device that blew up the car. From preliminary reports it is similar to the one we took from your car at the beach, Suzie.

"Now, the bad news. It appears that Maxine Small was one of the victims. Witness accounts put her near that car when it, or one close by, exploded. We aren't sure if there were any other victims, or if just cars were destroyed by the blast. It's being investigated now, and will take some time."

Marta turned white.

"That was meant for me, wasn't it? Her car was exactly like mine. Exactly. And, I helped her with her seat adjustment! I sat in her car; I adjusted the seat, and when I got out, we all walked across the street together. Anybody watching might have thought it was my car." She started shaking, and Shadow jumped off her lap to sit on the floor.

"Marta, we don't know that for sure. It's a coincidence, that's all."

"No, it isn't. Who would want that poor sweet lady dead? It's me they wanted to blow up. I don't believe in coincidences, anyway."

Suzie tightened her grip on Lady. "Marta, maybe it wasn't meant for you. Whoever has been trying to kill me, figured I'd be with you tonight."

He sighed again. "Ladies, we don't know. If someone was watching you, they may have assumed the car was yours. You said you were both helping Maxine with her car. We don't know who the target is at this point."

Shadow had regained his place on Marta's lap, and Suzie lessened her grip on Lady's fur.

"Still, that poor woman. She was such a delight to talk to. Oh dear."

"Marta, it may have been intended for her all along. Maybe she really pissed off the wrong person in her column. She's not exactly a sweet, grandmotherly type in print. She can get pretty cutting and dredge up some nasty things, including scandalous rumors.

"That said, for now, let's assume it was directed at one or both of you. Suzie, you will have an agent with you at all times. We need to ramp up this investigation. Marta, you, too. Now, it's late. I know it's going to be hard, but let's all try to get some sleep and regroup in the morning."

Chapter 53

HARRY'S VISIT TO Serge's attorney in town confirmed what the attorney in Venice had told him. He inherited Serge's house, acreage, and art studio along with a sizable amount of money. There was also a provision about Serge's share of his family's winery going to Harry, with the rest going to Francesca. Her family had been involved with the wine making process for decades.

His head was spinning when he left the attorney and headed into the hills toward the winery.

Francesca greeted him when he arrived, and they spent some time talking about Serge, his grandfather, and her family's involvement with the winery.

Harry filled her in on what he had just learned from the attorney. She had been listening and nodding. "I understand that, as I had a conversation with him as well. You now own 20% of this entire operation. We have quarterly meetings, and you will have a say in those meetings. Here, let me show you some records of past meetings. We can look at them over lunch."

They spent the next couple of hours going over the complete operation. Harry's head was no longer spinning. It was exploding. "Good night. I had no idea what all went into a business like this. I figured you grew grapes, crushed them, and you had wine. Whoa.

All I know about is designing gardens and outdoor spaces and growing plants."

"Yes, it is a big operation. But, it takes a lot of different people to keep it a viable business." Francesca was impressed with Harry's questions throughout the tour and her explanations of the business end. "You'll be a great asset to our business team. It's just too bad Serge isn't here to see this."

"He talked about his grandfather more than he talked about the winery. I don't know if he wasn't interested or was afraid because of the business he was involved in."

"I wondered the same thing, Harry. Was it really nasty business?"

Harry told her what he knew about Serge and forgeries. "I'm positive it was those forgeries that got him killed. I think the same guy that beat him up before probably came back. Serge had just told them he was finished forging paintings, and I don't think they liked it."

"Do you know who they are? Did he leave anything to give you or the police a clue?"

"Not really. The police are combing his laptop for hints. I didn't find anything to give me any information."

"Did you check his phone?"

"Yeah. Nothing there. Unless . . . "

"Unless, what?"

"I didn't look at his photos. Do you suppose the police did? They told me not to delete anything and would want to see it again. I wonder if he had any photos of the guy who came to his house that day. I have it with me. I wanted to know if you wanted to see it or if there were any calls that I didn't recognize. I thought maybe he called you or something."

"He hasn't called me in a very long time. I know he used to call his grandfather at least once a week. But, he's been gone almost a year now. Let's see the phone."

Harry took out Serge's phone, and they looked at his photo gallery. The most recent ones were of his latest forgeries. Nothing with any people in them.

"Well, it was worth a try."

After some more conversation, Harry left to go home. "Thanks for letting me take up your whole afternoon, Francesca. I'll definitely be back for the next meeting. I love learning new things."

Chapter 54

HARRY WAS ALMOST home when his phone rang. It was the police. "Can you come directly here to the station? We need to talk to you as soon as possible."

"Sure. I'm about 15 minutes away. What's up? Do you have more information?"

"We cannot say. Please come directly here."

The call ended quite abruptly, and Harry was worried. "I wonder what's going on. Surely, they don't think of me as a suspect, do they? If they found more information about Serge and his death, wouldn't they tell me?" His mind was working overtime, and he was talking and gesturing to no one in particular. He sped up, thinking if he got a speeding ticket, it would be worth it.

Arriving in less than 10 minutes, Harry rushed into the police station. The front desk clerk buzzed, and one of the detectives came out from a back room. "Glad you made it quickly. We still have the paintings Serge had given to you for safekeeping. There is an Interpol agent here who needs them and wants to question you. Okay?"

"Okay. But, what about? Am I being accused of anything? I only had those paintings because Serge gave them to me."

"Let's just go talk to the agent." The detective led the way into the large conference room. Harry thought to himself that at least it wasn't through the door that said Interrogation on it.

Seated at the table was the other detective and a man Harry had not seen before. The detective introduced the man to Harry. "This is Special Agent Pete Jensen from Interpol. He and some other agents have been tracking a forgery operation, and some things led him here. We've filled him in on Serge, from what we know. Now, he wants to ask you some questions."

Harry nodded and sat in the chair the detective indicated.

"I'll try to answer what I can, Special Agent Jensen. I don't think I know much, however."

Pete smiled. "Call me Pete. I have read everything you've told the detectives. Now, I want to hear it directly from you. Something may have popped into your mind since you last talked with them. Why don't you start from how long you've known Serge? Tell me about what you know of his painting business, and I'll ask questions when you're finished. Okay?"

Harry took a breath and filled Pete in on everything he could. When he finished with his visit to the attorney and to the winery, he looked at the detectives and then at Pete. "I have questions, too. Probably similar to yours."

Pete nodded. "I'm sure. Let me start. From what you've said Serge told you recently, he was trying to get out of forging paintings. You mentioned the paper he used and some grass or weeds in the crates. The paper he used in packing the crates is one reason I'm in this area. You see, my best friend from college grew up here. I came to visit him several times. One of the bundles of packing papers had a name of a business I recognized from here. I didn't know if that same business name was in other places, but it was a good starting point. The more I dug, the more it led to this area.

"We've been looking at several forgeries for quite some time. Right now I can't go into all the details, as it's still an ongoing investigation. But, I knew I was getting close for the Italian connection. I just examined the crate of paintings Serge left for you to take care of, and he's good. Damn good. I'm positive he's one lead.

"Now, we just need to figure out how he's connected to Paris, southern France, and to San Francisco."

"Wait." Harry interrupted. "Didn't Serge go to art school in Paris? Could that be the connection? I just now remembered he mentioned France and Paris."

"It could be. Any idea when that would have been?"

Harry thought and finally said he really didn't know. "I only know I met him about seven years ago, and we became good friends. He was already finished with school or at least mostly finished. The reason he apparently moved here was to avoid some guy in Paris. But, it didn't work. They found him somehow."

"Well, that fits with some of the things we're investigating. That helps. Now, you mentioned a couple of things I want to ask you about. One, you said Serge put a symbol somewhere on the paintings. Do you know where?"

"I think he said he put a key, sort of like a skeleton key, by the signature. I should have asked more about that. At the time, it seemed kind of silly to me. Just like the packing paper. Why? Did you find something?"

"Our lab did, indeed, find a skeleton key painted on one of the paintings. They'll definitely look for that on the others. Do you know why he did that? Do you think he just wanted someone to know the paintings were definite forgeries?"

"I'm sorry. I was so wrapped up in my new clients, I didn't ask enough questions of Serge. It apparently was important enough to him that he mentioned it to me. But, why? I don't know. Damn. If I had paid more attention, Serge might still be alive." Dejectedly, Harry put his head in his hands.

"Don't beat yourself up. It's enough that you told us about the key. We'll figure out the rest. It's not your fault. We want to catch his killer and put this forgery organization out of business. Anything and everything helps. For now, let's all talk about this in the morning. Maybe I'll have some news by then. And, if you think of anything more, let me know. Okay?" He handed Harry a business card.

Chapter 55

IN SAN FRANCISCO no one slept peacefully. Marta and Suzie both tossed and turned all night. At one point, Lady jumped in bed with Suzie, pressing her cold nose into Suzie's face, and Shadow stayed as close to Marta as he could get.

Agents Mitchell and Hansen took turns watching the dark house and listening for anything out of the ordinary. About 5 a.m. Greg took a call from Clark, and it was confirmed that Suzie would have a visible bodyguard with her at all times. Another one would be invisible, but nearby. At this point, it wasn't clear who was the intended target. For that reason, another agent would be assigned to Marta, as well.

"Greg, everyone who had any direct contact with any of the forgeries is dead, except for Suzie and Marta, who both dealt with different aspects of the forgeries. Oh, and the Ascots. That's more than troublesome. Pete has just learned about a man who we think may be the forger of the paintings. He was working for someone, and Pete is working that angle as we speak. I'll have to fill you in on that later. For now, keep Suzie and Marta safe. I'll call Marta later.

"We'd like for Suzie to go to her shop and conduct business as usual. She needs to do the same things she always does. Make sure an agent and her dog are with her. Okay? I'd feel better if she stayed at Marta's for the time being and if at least one of you was there, too. Let's touch base later tonight. Call me anytime. Talk to you then."

Agent Mitchell filled Agent Hansen and Marta in on the plan as Suzie and Lady came into the kitchen.

"Guess what? The place where I got Lady called me back. Lady started in training as a police dog, sniffing for drugs. They already told me she has quite the nose. But, she lacked the fierceness they needed at the time. So, one of the trainers took her and gave her to his aunt. She needed a companion, as she suffered from a mild form of epilepsy. Lady could sense an episode, and the aunt would take her meds before she had a full-blown attack. Then, when the aunt died, Lady came to the shelter. She had only been there three weeks when I got her. Now we know why she's so good."

"Suzie, that makes perfect sense. I knew she had to have some special training. Lucky you."

"I know."

"Okay. Let's all keep one another informed of where you'll be and what you're doing. Suzie, you and I will head to your shop about the same time you would normally get there. Marta, what do you have planned for today and for the week?"

"First I have a question. Do we know for sure if Maxine Small was in the car that exploded?"

"Yes, by preliminary reports, she was. We'll have confirmation later in the week. Why?"

"I just wondered if we should do something for her family or something."

"Let's wait until all is confirmed and the police have finished their investigation. Okay?"

"I suppose. I just feel so bad for her family. Does she have a family?"

"Marta, I'm not sure. I'll check, and then we can decide what to do. Now, what are your plans for the day?"

Marta nodded. "Today, just office work. I'm ironing out all the final details for the next Italy trip. Then, later this week, I need to meet with a last minute addition to my next tour in Venice. He hasn't been to any of my informational meetings, so I need to bring him up to date on what is expected of him and what he can expect on this tour. We're meeting at a coffee shop not all that far from Suzie's shop at 11 a.m. tomorrow or the next day. I need to check my calendar.

"It will probably take about an hour. I have no idea if he's a seasoned traveler or not. Hopefully, I won't have to go over basic Travel 101 with him. Do you want me to cancel that or change it? I can come to Suzie's when I finish with him."

"Yes, see if you can move that up. I'd like for us to see what happens today. Okay, everybody. Pay attention, and stay safe."

Chapter 56

IN ANOTHER PART of San Francisco, he didn't sleep well either. First, he paced. Then, he picked up a crystal vase and hurled it at one of the paintings on the wall in his office. The gaping hole in the Renoir didn't register with him, nor did the spectacular crash as the vase hit the corner of a desk and shattered into a million sparkling pieces.

All he could see was his master plan. And, it was beginning to fall apart. He could just hear Dixie admonishing him, and he didn't want to be on the receiving end of that. Good thing she was busy with one of her thugs.

It was just a matter of time before the police came back and asked more questions. That didn't set well, either.

Picking up his phone, he made yet another call.

"Carlo, you idiot, where the hell are you? What the hell is going on? Have you given my instructions to that no-good painter, Serge? I hope you can at least follow these instructions, you bumbling idiot. Don't even think about screwing this up. I need him to paint one more piece before we get rid of him. Now, damn it, answer your phone, if you know what's good for you." This call, like the three before it, went right to voicemail. "Damn imbeciles. Can't even answer a phone.

"Nothing is going as planned. I'm done dealing with incompetent idiots. It's time to take matters into my own hands." He spoke to the empty room, gesturing with his cup of morning coffee. "I'll show that woman.

"Time to call the newspaper and inquire about the occupant of the car. I'm hearing some things I don't like." His call to the paper revealed nothing. No one would confirm or deny if there was anyone in the car that blew up, nor would they speculate on who might have been in it.

Next, he placed a call to George, who answered on the first ring. "Hey, Boss. Did you hear about the car blowing up in front of that mansion and all those people? Good job, huh? What do you mean, who was in the car? It was her car. Of course it was her. Who else would it be?"

He interrupted George's babbling. "I want absolute confirmation of the body, and I don't care how you find out. I have good reason to believe it wasn't the blonde. In fact, I'm positive it wasn't."

"How can that be? I saw her get in it. What do you want me to do, Boss?"

"I don't care what you do or how you do it. Just find out who died. Got it?" He ended the call before George could respond.

"Okay. Enough messing around. If she isn't already dead, she'll die soon. I'll personally see to it."

Chapter 57

SUZIE, LADY, AND Greg left in his car. Marta made a phone call and left a message to see if she could meet the new traveler today rather than later in the week. In a few minutes he returned her call, and they set a time for today. Gathering her papers and forms, she decided to add her small recorder at the last minute. On more than one occasion it had come in handy. She didn't have time to wait for one of the agents to return to go with her.

Placing a call to Clark, she left a voicemail, mentioning she was going without one of the agents. "Clark, I'll be extra careful. Talk to you later."

The cab dropped her off in front of one of her favorite coffee shops in the area known as North Beach. She sent a text to Greg to let him know where she was and that she would come to Suzie's when she was finished here. She walked in and greeted the owner, ordered her usual, and found a table towards the back. Looking around, she saw no one who might be who she was meeting. "Hey, Luigi, I'm meeting someone today, and I don't know what he looks like. If anyone asks about a travel lady or is looking for someone connected to a tour to Italy, will you please direct them my way?"

"Sure thing. No one new in here so far."

Marta worked on some finishing touches for the tour as almost an hour passed. People came and went, but no one inquired about a travel lady. Then, like the others in the coffee shop, she looked up when fire trucks and an ambulance blared past outside. Finally, she decided to pack up her things. "Guess he's a no show. Bye, Luigi. See you later." She packed her folders and papers into her oversized bag, put it over her shoulder, and headed out the door.

Stepping out into the unusually bright sunlight, she looked down into her bag as she walked, trying to find her sunglasses. From behind, someone grabbed her arm. Tightly. Flashes of Venice immediately came to mind. She tried to turn around. "Excuse me. Please let go of my arm." The grip tightened. More, ugly thoughts flew through her mind. "Will you please let go? You're hurting me." The sidewalk was empty, and she saw no one nearby that could help.

Just then, under her arm, she felt a prick in her side. "Ouch." The prick became more intense as it dawned on her it could be a knife. Thinking she had to do something, she took a deep breath just like Clark had taught her, she dropped her bag, gathered what strength she had, stepped on her attacker's foot, and whirled around to knee him in the groin. Taking him by surprise, she hit her mark on his instep and close to her mark on his groin. He made a whoosh and a gasp as he let go of Marta's arm. That was all the time she needed to run the part of a block back into the coffee shop.

"Luigi, help me." She practically flew through the door.

Luigi came around the counter. "What happened, Miss Marta? You look scared."

Breathing heavily now, her eyes darting back and forth, Marta looked out the window. "Is there a man out there? A big guy? He grabbed me and stuck something in my side. I don't know what he wanted. Oh crap. I dropped my bag. That's my life right now." She ran her hand through her blonde hair and tried to calm her racing heart.

"I'll get it. You stay here. Franco, keep an eye on Miss Marta."

Luigi came back a couple of minutes later with Marta's bag and a small knife. "I found these on the sidewalk just down at the end of the block. But, I didn't see anybody around at all. He's long gone. Probably a druggie who wanted your purse. You should see if anything is missing, and we should call the cops. Maybe they can get fingerprints from the knife, even though I touched it."

"You're right, Luigi. I wasn't paying attention, and that was stupid of me. I'll report it to the police, but I don't even have a description of the guy, other than he was bigger than me and strong. He'll just go find some other purse to grab." Marta was disgusted with herself, especially in light of all that had happened lately.

"Here, you sit and have a coffee. Relax. Okay?" Luigi had set a large cup of coffee and a biscotti in front of her as more sirens roared past the coffee shop. Luigi wrapped the knife in a plastic bag and gave it to Marta.

"Thanks, Luigi." Marta sipped the coffee and looked through her things. "It doesn't look like he wanted my paperwork, and he probably didn't see my wallet or any money." She turned on her recorder and was about to record the attack to give to the police, when a man limped toward her table. "Excuse me. I was supposed to meet a lady about a travel trip to Venice. I'm late for that meeting. Would you happen to be her?" His voice was hardly more than a raspy whisper.

Marta looked up into the face of an older man. Stooped over, his dark cap was low on his head, straggly gray hair flowing out from under it. He didn't remove his hat nor his ultra-dark sunglasses. Marta was positive he had on make-up. The way he mumbled and his demeanor had Marta wondering if he would be strong enough for the trip.

Chapter 58

SHE SMILED. "YES, I am the organizer of the trip. I'm
sorry I'm a little rattled. A thug tried to grab my purse a few minutes ago. Let's see, your name is Harry Madsen, right?"

He nodded without speaking.

"Okay. Please, have a seat. I need to go over the details with
you." She tried to clear the attack from her mind and focus on her
client, as she pulled out a folder. She turned it toward him, thinking he would take off his sunglasses so he could see it better. He
didn't.

Slowing her ragged breathing and her racing mind, she tried
to concentrate on Mr. Madsen. Explaining the trip, mentioning the
requirements, and telling him he would be receiving a complete
trip packet in the next week, she felt she was going too fast for the
older man.

He sat, not really engaging. He nodded when she asked him
some questions, mumbled at others, and had no questions of his
own. She noticed at times he seemed disinterested, and yet he
seemed to focus on her face from under his cap. Thinking she
could get him to open up, she asked him about art. "Do you have
some favorite artists or artwork you're hoping to see?" He just
shrugged.

It ran through her mind that she should just stop this process and tell him the trip was full. If he was going to be this noncommittal for the entire trip, it wasn't going to be fun for anybody. She thought to herself that this had been a complete waste of time and made a silent bet he wouldn't even show up for the trip.

"Is there anything I can do to make your trip better for you?" Again, a shrug and a grunted answer.

"No. I just want to start."

Since his answers didn't make a lot of sense, she was glad she kept her recorder on, even though it was in her bag.

"Are we done?" He shifted impatiently in his chair.

"Almost. One final paper to sign and then I will need your entire payment." Marta turned the disclaimer form toward him, and he scribbled his name, hardly touching the paper. She thought to herself that his hands looked considerably younger than what she first thought by looking at his face. "You might want to read it first." Marta was positive this was the oddest person she had ever taken on a tour.

Mr. Madsen mumbled something as he pushed the paper back toward Marta. "I need to get my checkbook out of my car. You do take checks?"

"At this stage of the process all I take is credit cards. Sorry." She thought to herself that she had already told him that. Wasn't he listening? Maybe he didn't have a credit card. She hoped that was the case and she could tell him goodbye.

"Oh. My wallet is in my car, too. If you come with me, I can pay you in full. My car is one block away." Mr. Madsen pointed in the direction of Suzie's shop, so Marta figured she may as well head that way, take his credit card payment, and then continue on to Suzie's shop. She'd fill the detectives in on her strange day.

"Sure. Let's go." Marta gathered up her things and waved to Luigi. "Bye. Thanks again, Luigi. I'm going to call the police as soon as I finish here. See you tomorrow."

They exited the coffee shop and headed in the direction he had pointed. Marta noticed he walked better now than when he first came by her table. She tried to ask him a few more questions to get a better feel for what he wanted from the trip, but he just mumbled. Finally, Marta quit asking. At the end of the first block, they stopped for the traffic light, and Marta turned to him. "Where did you say your car was? We've already come one block."

"Just down here." He pointed in the direction they were headed. She thought to herself she was glad Suzie's shop and the agents were around the next corner. This guy was definitely weird. They crossed the street and continued down the block as one more police car roared past, siren blasting. He visibly flinched.

"Did you park along the street or in this parking ramp?" Marta motioned to the ramp's entrance as he kept walking past it.

"Come this way. Not far. Let's go, my dear." This time his words were clear, not whispered, as he pointed in the direction they were walking.

Something about the way he said those last words set off alarm bells for Marta. *Where have I heard such a syrupy voice before? Think, Marta, think. It's not good, but it's not coming to me.* The alarm bells in her head kept ringing. She hesitated.

"Come with me, dear. We can't be late."

More alarm bells, this time clanging loudly.

Shaking her head, she stopped in the middle of the sidewalk. "On second thought, I am late for another appointment and have to go. I'll call you to get your payment information." She turned slightly away from him, ready to head in another direction. Those alarm bells in her head were now clanging double-time.

"Oh, I don't think so." The sickening sweet voice now had a hard edge to it. He reached out to grab Marta just as she glimpsed another man quickly approaching them.

Chapter 59

"MISS MARTA, YOU forgot your glasses." Franco, from Luigi's Coffee Shop was weaving in and out of people on the sidewalk, hurrying to catch up with Marta and Mr. Madsen.

That was all it took for Marta to whirl around, lose the grip Mr. Madsen had on her sleeve, and stumble toward Franco. With a surprised look on his face, Franco reached out to steady her. "Are you okay? Luigi said to hurry and get these to you. You might need them."

Looking back at where Mr. Madsen had been standing, Marta saw only others stepping off the sidewalk and into the street. Madsen was nowhere to be seen. "Did you see which way Mr. Madsen went, Franco?"

"Who?"

"The man who I was talking to in Luigi's. The one who left with me? The older guy."

"No, Miss Marta. I only saw you standing with all these other people." Franco gestured to the group now on the other side of the street.

"Franco, you may have just saved my life. Thank you."

With a puzzled look on his face, Franco shook his head. "I don't understand."

"Me neither, really.

Chapter 60

MARTA AND FRANCO chatted a couple more minutes while Marta kept watching for Mr. Madsen, then she thanked him again. "Be sure to tell Luigi what happened. Please ask him if he remembers anything unusual about Mr. Madsen, too. I have a good description of what he looks like since I spent some time talking to him, but he may remember something I didn't. I owe you, Franco."

"Just glad to help, Miss Marta. See you around. Be careful."

Marta took a good look around. No one resembling Mr. Madsen was anywhere near her. She decided to tell the agents about the attack and to call the police about the knife when she got to Suzie's shop. But, when she turned the corner, she noticed a fire truck sitting in the street with its lights flashing. Three police cars sat directly in front of it. "That's never a good thing." She took another quick look around at people as she hurried toward the scene.

Approaching one policeman, she noticed the glass by the front door of Suzie's shop resembled a large spider web. Since it was a special kind of glass, it wasn't really broken, but totally destroyed. "Officer, what's going on?"

The officer stepped toward Marta. "Miss, please stay back. This is a crime scene."

"What? What crime? My friend owns this shop, and I was coming to see her. What about the man who was with her? I need to talk to him, to them." Marta stepped toward the door, and the officer stepped in front of her.

"Let's go over here and talk. Who are you, and why were you coming to see the shop owner?"

Marta followed, but kept looking over her shoulder at Suzie's shop. "What happened? Was anybody hurt? Can I go see them?"

"Ma'am, please." As the officer was talking and gently moving Marta away from in front of the shop, a large, black, SUV pulled up to the curb. Agent Hansen and another man got out, approached the officer, discreetly showing him their badges, and nodding at Marta, who was trying to get a better look at Suzie's shop. When she recognized the agents, she motioned toward the front door.

"Jon, do you know what's going on? Why is the glass broken?"

"One minute, Marta." He continued his conversation with the police officer and then turned to Marta. "Okay. Let's go to your house. We've had some developments here and need to keep you safe."

"Wait. I want to see Suzie. Where is she?"

"She's at the hospital right now. We can't go there just yet. Let's get you out of here. Okay?" Jon had taken Marta's arm and was walking toward the SUV. Marta continued to look over her shoulder at the destroyed front door and window.

"I don't get it. The hospital? What happened?"

"Come. Let's go. We need to get you out of here now." He opened the door and helped Marta inside, as the SUV was already pulling away from the curb. "Take the long route. I'll notify our tail what we're doing.

"Marta, I'll explain everything we know as soon as we get to your house. I know you have questions, and I'll try to answer them."

Marta took a deep breath. "You'll want to know about what happened to me today, too. I'm beginning to think I'm as much of a target as Suzie. And, I want to know what you guys know about Thomas Smith. He's involved."

Chapter 61

AFTER SEVERAL MINUTES and a circuitous route home to Marta's, the SUV pulled into her garage, and the driver made a phone call. Marta recognized Agent Stu Thompson as the driver. As she and Jon went inside, they were greeted by Lady's wagging tail and Shadow's meowing. Setting her bag down, Marta rubbed Lady's ears and picked up a purring Shadow. "Hey guys. I hope you've had a better day than the rest of us."

Jon had made a quick tour of Marta's house. Both he and Stu came into the kitchen to join Marta. "Looks like you have some friends there." Shadow nestled on Marta's lap, and Lady sat as close as she could to Marta's chair.

"Okay, what the hell is going on? Is Suzie okay? Was her shop broken into?"

Both agents sat down at the table with Marta. "Let's start from this morning when Greg and Suzie went to her shop. She received another phone call about yet another painting someone wanted to sell. It was from a man, unlisted number, who said he would be there at five o'clock today with the painting. He said he heard she paid cash for paintings, and he wanted cash for his."

Marta nodded. "That's too coincidental. Right?"

"Right. All sorts of red flags for Greg. He called for back-up in the shop, had other agents and local police on alert in the area, and he and Suzie were going over the plan. Ian and Clark had been notified as well.

"Then, about 20 or 30 minutes after the call came in, all hell broke loose."

"What happened?"

"Someone shot at the front window and door. You saw the mess in front. We're pretty certain it wasn't from close range and probably meant to disrupt, based on what happened next. We'll know more when ballistics is finished examining the bullet and the door. Needless to say, it was loud and probably quite the shock to both Greg and Suzie. They weren't expecting anything like that, and they weren't expecting anyone with a painting until closer to five o'clock."

Marta nodded and continued to scratch Lady's ears.

"According to protocol, he called in to report the shot, grabbed Suzie, and hustled them both out the back. Agents or local guys were supposed to be watching the alley and the back door. We still aren't clear on where they were or exactly what happened, but none of our guys were there. They were both sitting ducks."

"No! Are they okay?" Marta's response had both animals reacting.

"Both are in surgery right now. Greg took a direct hit to his chest area, but was wearing a vest. The bullet penetrated some flesh just to the side of the vest, probably when he turned to protect Suzie. We'll get updates from the hospital shortly."

"What about Suzie?"

"Marta, we're not completely sure. We do know she was hit twice. One bullet hit her in the head and one entered her side, but we don't know the extent of the damage, and she's in surgery as well."

Marta gasped. Lady stuck her cold nose into Marta's hand. After a couple of seconds, Marta looked up from Lady. "What's going to happen? Who did this? What else do you know?"

Before either could answer, Jon's phone rang, and he stepped away to answer. When Stu's phone rang, he sat down at the table as Marta continued to pet both animals. They both finished their calls and sat down by Marta.

"We have some news. Like we first thought, the front window was shot by a rifle, not close by. The police are still looking into possible locations. Ballistics will be able to tell what kind of rifle from the bullet they recovered. We caught a break on the alley shootings of Greg and Suzie. A shop owner just down the block had stepped into the alley from his shop to take a smoke break. When he heard the loud noise from the first shot out front, he turned to hurry back inside and just happened to catch a glimpse of someone on the roof of the building directly behind Suzie's. When he looked up, he noticed a flash of light coming from that direction and thought the person had a flashlight. Then, he heard some popping noises and ran back inside. After securing his back door, he called 911.

"That's about all the police got from him. He was pretty shaken up when the police told him two people had been shot. The good news is, the bakery at the other end of the block has a security camera in the alley. We have that footage now. Jon, what do you know?"

"More good news. The police were able to quickly determine a possible location for the rifle shot and narrowed it down to a couple of buildings. Inspecting the roof of one of those, they discovered a shell casing. It's a start."

Jon looked at Marta. "I heard you say something when you got in the car. Talk to us."

Chapter 62

MARTA SMILED AT both agents. "This will pale in comparison to Suzie and Greg being shot. But, my day has been anything but normal." She sighed.

"Okay. Start from the beginning. And, don't leave out your comment about Thomas Smith."

Marta nodded and replayed her day for the agents, starting with the attempted mugging, giving them the plastic bag with the knife, and ending with getting away from who she was positive was Thomas Smith. "At first, I didn't even think of those two incidents being connected. I figured it was just a brazen thief with a knife trying to grab a purse in broad daylight. Now, I'm having second thoughts about that. It's still puzzling to me why he'd grab my purse and then let go when I kneed him. He didn't put up any fight, and he was bigger than me."

"Perhaps he was a distraction or maybe someone else was supposed to be around to help him. Do you think the coffee shop owner, Luigi, has outdoor security cameras?"

"I think so, but I was at least two or three doors down from him when the guy grabbed my bag. Maybe one of the other shops has cameras."

"We'll check. And, we'll get this knife to forensics. Good work on Luigi's part. Now, let's go over the details about the man who was claiming to be on your tour. When did he sign up? What do you know about him? Can you describe him well enough for a sketch artist, and is there anything else you can remember?"

Marta went over the details, checking her notebook for any facts about Mr. Madsen. "I don't usually accept new people this late. I keep a waiting list, but they are required to come to my introductory meetings so they know what is going to happen. This time, I allowed Mr. Madsen. At the time, I thought I really shouldn't do that. But, I did it anyway. Never again. I still don't know how he would have made it on my list. That puzzles me."

Marta had been scribbling as she talked and showed her drawing to the agents. "This is pretty much what he looked like. Only, at one point, I could have sworn he was wearing make-up, and his hands appeared to be younger looking than his face. His voice changed, too. He mumbled a lot in the coffee shop, but once outside, his syrupy, sing-song voice really reminded me of Thomas Smith. No, it was more than that! It was Thomas Smith. I'd bet on it. But, with a disguise. I might have caught something on my recorder, even though it was in my bag." Marta pulled it out and handed it to Jon.

"Do you think I'm as much of a target as Suzie?"

"It's beginning to look that way. For some reason, whoever this is doesn't want either of you around. With Suzie, it's more than likely because of that Picasso forgery. For you, we're not sure yet."

Marta's head came up sharply. "Wait a minute. Suzie bought the painting, but I told her I thought it was a forgery. I even talked to the place in Carmel in length about it. Could that be related somehow? Or, is he in cahoots with the auction place in Carmel?" She stood up and started to pace around the kitchen. "Thomas Smith has so many paintings, some which I think could be real. They look that good. Yet I know for a fact, the genuine ones are hanging in famous museums and galleries.

"Or, are they? And, that's not really enough to try to kill me. Is it? I mean, I never directly talked to him about his paintings. How does he know me, anyway?

"Then, there's Milan and Venice. How do they fit into this? Is he connected to those, too? Is he somehow connected to the gallery owner in Venice? If I remember correctly, his name was Sir Antonio Furst."

Both agents had been listening to Marta as she threw out suggestions and questions. Jon spoke first. "Marta, all great questions. And, right now, all questions with no answers. I think we need to talk to Clark and Ian."

Stu's phone rang again. "Yeah. Okay. We'll be there."

"Let's take a trip to the hospital. Both Suzie and Greg are out of surgery. I don't think they'll be able to talk, but at least we can see them."

$\mathcal{C}$hapter 63

WHEN HIS DRIVER let him off at the side entrance, and he came barreling in the mansion, Dixie knew something was wrong. Really wrong. He looked like he could explode at any minute. *I'm going to have to fix things. Again. This time for good.*

Stomping through the first floor toward his office and cursing under his breath, he plopped down on the soft, brown, leather sofa. With his head in his hands, his anger continued to boil. "Why do these idiots screw up time after time? It was a simple job. Just shoot the damn front window; don't leave any evidence, and get the hell out of the country." Practically shouting at the slim woman sitting across from him, he stood up, walked to his giant desk, and slammed his fist down on it. "What the hell is so hard about that?"

She nodded and started to speak when he interrupted her. "And, George has screwed up for the last time. Stupid man can't do anything right. First, he was supposed to eliminate the targets with bombs. Bombs. Bombs kill people. But, no. He made a mess of that. And, for what? The targets didn't even die. Nothing's hard about a bomb, for God's sake. Damn it!

"And, it doesn't get any easier than to kill two people in an alley. Who knows if they're dead or alive? George sure doesn't. They're in the hospital, but I can't find out anything." He swore under his breath and slammed the other fist on the desk.

She watched and listened. *This isn't good. He's losing it right in front of me. Time for Plan B. He's become a liability.* She would take care of things, like she always did. Then it would be finished here.

"How many lives does that stupid, blonde woman have anyway? She should have been scared shitless by the guy I hired to snatch her purse. She should have been running away. She was in my sight, and I was all ready to put a bullet in her head. But, no. The idiot let her get the best of him. He ran away like a scared rabbit when she kicked him. What a pansy.

"So, I had to improvise. Then, she got lucky when the waiter came running down the street. One more block and she would have been history. This is ridiculous, but she's just run out of luck."

He stood up and paced. Looking at Dixie, he shook his head. "Did you see the news? It appears the police have some security footage they say is the shooter. Great! Well, that's just too bad for poor old George, because that's the last anybody will see of him."

Dixie stood up. She had heard enough. "Okay. Here's what's going to happen." She outlined the plan and handed him the phone. "Call him now."

When he hung up, he looked at Dixie. "He took the bait. He'll meet at the usual spot to collect his payoff and his ticket to England. He's not expecting you."

"Alright. I'll finish him. Then, I'm going to the hospital where the blonde will surely come to visit her poor, little friend. When she does, I'll take care of both of them. This whole mess just needs to be finished. Get your things in order." *It's time for me to get back to London.*

Dixie went upstairs to change.

Chapter 64

IN ITALY, PETE wrapped up one part of his investigation, convinced that Serge was the forger for most, if not all, of the paintings they had been investigating. The lab had found the key Harry mentioned on all the paintings they had. There were still some missing pieces, however. They had no murder suspect for Serge's death. The local guys would have to continue to work on that one, using what few fingerprints they were able to pull from Serge's home. And, they had no clear path to whomever had been ordering and paying Serge to forge paintings. That was disturbing to Pete.

Any phone calls or texts were traced to burn phones, so no luck there. No emails. Nothing. On his last day at the police headquarters, Pete handed off copies of his investigation to the lead detective. "Good luck, and keep me informed. I'd really like to figure out who was behind this, but for now we'll wait. Something will drop. It always does." They all said goodbye, and Pete was out the door when one of the detectives came charging after him.

"Get back in here. His phone is ringing."

Running back into the office, another detective held up the phone that had been in Serge's things. He pointed to it as Pete nodded and hit the speaker button. "Hello."

"Who is this? Where's Serge?" The voice on the other end was curt, with a slight British accent.

"This is Pete. I'm Serge's new agent. If you want Serge to continue to work for you, you'll have to talk to me." Pete played a hunch this was the man who ordered Serge to paint for him. If not, he'd find out soon enough.

"I only talk to Serge. Not some excuse for a go-between."

"That's fine. But, if that's the case, then Serge is finished painting for you."

"You don't tell me when he's finished. I call the shots. If Serge knows what's good for him, he'll get my paintings finished on time. Now, where the hell is he?"

"Like I said, you talk only to me now. If that's not good enough, I'll hang up, and you'll never find Serge again. Goodbye." Pete looked at one detective, whose eyes had widened. The other detective was trying to get a fix on where the call had originated and motioned for Pete to keep the caller talking.

"No, wait. Don't hang up. I need to pick up a painting Serge was to have finished for me. My courier will be there today. Let Serge know it better be perfect, or he'll be sorry."

"His work is always perfect. What time can he expect the courier?"

"He'll be there in a couple of hours. If Serge doesn't cooperate, he'll have to answer to me."

"I'll make sure he's there with the painting. He'll expect payment at that time as well. By the way, his fees have gone up."

"I don't think so. You tell him he's in no position to call the shots. I can have him arrested and sent to where he'll rot in jail for the rest of his life. Or worse, I'll send someone to take care of him. Got it?"

Pete started to ask another question to keep him on the call longer, but he had hung up. He looked at the one detective. "Damn. I'm sorry. I thought I could keep him talking."

The detective looked at his screen and then at Pete. "We got close. The call was routed around the world, but I lost it somewhere in California."

"I'll let Ian and Clark know. We had some other leads that put us in San Francisco, and this may originate there as well. Thanks. Now, I need to get out to Serge's and meet that courier. Who wants to come with me?"

Chapter 65

PETE AND TWO detectives sat and waited in Serge's house. All the crime tape and evidence of any investigation was removed.

"We don't know if this courier is involved in any way other than just being a courier service. For now, let's assume he's part of the operation and treat him as such. I'll answer the door, let him know I am Serge's agent, and tell him the crate is in Serge's studio. Then, I'll give him the option of waiting here or coming with me to the studio to get the crate from Serge. He won't know Serge isn't there. I want one of you inside, unseen, and the other one in the studio. Okay?

"It should be fairly obvious if he is only a courier or if he knows what's going on. We'll have to play that by ear as it develops. My hope is that he will have a way he contacts whomever is ordering these forgeries. Any questions?"

Both detectives nodded their heads, and everyone took their place, awaiting the courier. It didn't take long for a dark van to pull into Serge's driveway, and after a couple of minutes, a burly man, dressed in dark gray, stepped out and looked around. Pete watched as he made his way toward the front door, noticing a bulge on his left side. Whispering to the detective in the kitchen, he motioned. "He's armed."

When the knock came, Pete waited a few seconds before answering the door, surprising the man. "Hey, where's Serge? Who are you?" Pete immediately noticed the man tensing as his eyes took in Pete and the surroundings. "I'm here to talk to Serge. Where is he?"

Pete stuck out his hand to the man in the doorway. "I'm his new agent, Pete. Serge's in his studio. May I help you?"

"I don't talk to nobody but Serge. He's got paintings for me. I need to talk to him now." Filling the doorway and trying to intimidate Pete, he took a step into the house. Pete stepped aside to let him in. "Take me to Serge. I gotta get those paintings and give him a message from the Boss." As he came further into the room, Pete saw his right hand flex and his stance change.

"Sure. No problem. What's the message?"

"None of your business. Now get outta my way. Where is he?"

"He's in his studio with the paintings. This way." Pete motioned toward the building just outside the side door.

Nodding his head toward the door, the man gestured. "You go first. And, don't think of doin' nothin'."

Pete stood his ground. "Let's get something straight first. Serge's fees have gone up, and I need to make sure he gets paid before I give you the paintings."

"I told you. I don't deal with you. He doesn't make the rules. Take me to Serge. Now." He had pulled out his weapon and aimed it at Pete.

Pete held up his hands. "Sure. No problem. This way." He started to lead the way to the studio through the door off the kitchen. With his back to the man, he opened the side door, and heard the detective. "Hands up. Police. Drop the weapon."

The big guy turned around and fired in the direction of the detective, just as Pete pulled his weapon and aimed it at his back. The detective was quick, and his aim was perfect. The man went down, a red stain forming on the front of his gray shirt. Pete took a step toward him as the guy tried to fire another shot, this one at Pete's face. Again, the detective was quick and fired one more shot as the guy lay on the floor. No more movement from him.

"I wasn't going to kill him, but when he started shooting, I had no choice." The detective looked at Pete and at the second detective who came running in from the studio with his weapon drawn.

"That's okay. We weren't going to get any information out of him, anyway. And, it's obvious he's part of the operation. He was here to harm Serge, possibly kill him, and take the paintings. His boss will be wondering if he's completed his job, however. Wonder if he has a cell phone." Pete put on a pair of gloves and started going through the dead man's pockets. "Bingo. Now, let's see what it can tell us. Then, we need to call both your boss and mine. This guy can go to the morgue."

Chapter 66

PETE SPENT SOME time looking through the dead guy's phone, finding several calls and texts. "Huh. It's odd he wouldn't have a password or a lock on this."

"Maybe he didn't know how, or maybe he never thought about it."

"Yeah, that's possible. It's not a new phone. He certainly receives more calls than he sends, and they seem to come from three common numbers. He texts only one of those numbers though. We should head to the station, send a text to this number, and see what happens. Someone is probably waiting to hear from him."

The medical examiner's van and two policemen had arrived and were dealing with the body. "We'll get someone in here to clean this up and let Harry know not to come here for a while. Do you think anybody else will be coming?"

"Who knows. We're heading to the station now, and we'll let you know if we find anything that tells us there might be someone else." The detectives and Pete left.

Once at the station, the phone was dusted for fingerprints, and Pete sent a text similar to ones he had read on the phone. *Got the paintings. Took care of Serge. What's next?* "Okay. Let's see if we get a response. If it doesn't come quickly, I'll take the phone with me and let you know when I get one." Pete packed up his gear once again and was heading out the door when the phone beeped.

Setting it on the table so the detectives could see it, they read the message.

Bring the paintings to the apartment and wait there.

"Damn. That doesn't help us." Pete looked up at the detectives.

"Wait a minute. Maybe one of our IT guys can figure out a location, especially if this guy has been to an apartment around here." The detective left to find their head technical man.

After several minutes the tech guy looked up. "Well, there's good news and bad news."

"Okay. Give it all to us."

"First, the good news. The texts all go to a single phone. I can work with it and send another partial text message telling them I dropped the phone, and it's been damaged. I'll tell them I couldn't quite get all of the previous text. That may make them call us, and we can go from there. Does anybody know his name? The bad news, if we don't figure out where the text is going, don't get a call back, and don't know where the apartment is, we're back to square one."

"Why don't you send a partial text, and let's see what happens? My guess is, he's a hired thug and not the brightest bulb. I wouldn't use big words or too much detail. Okay?" Pete motioned to one of the detectives. "Can you find out his name?" He nodded and left the room.

"Okay. Here goes. In essence, I'm going to say I dropped my phone, and it is not working well. I'll leave out some characters and scramble others. If the person on the other end is tech savvy, we'll have a problem. If not, we may just get lucky." He went to work creating and sending a message.

The detective came back into the room with the dead man's wallet. "Got this out of his pocket when they were clearing the crime scene. It's been dusted for prints. According to this, his name is Luis Garza, and he lives in town here. That is, if this is real. I'm having his prints run against all the databases to verify everything. It might take a while to get a hit, though."

As he was speaking, a lady from the forensics lab knocked on the door and entered. "You guys are lucky. These fingerprints show up all over the place. He's wanted by Interpol, the French police, the FBI in the States, and everybody else including God. He goes by several different names."

"Thanks, Gabriella. I need to call my boss at Interpol. This is beginning to make sense, but what we need is a connection to a bigger fish." As Pete was speaking, the phone rang. Looking at the number, he noticed it said private. "Start the trace. I'll try to sound like I have a problem with my voice and see what we get."

Chapter 67

IN SAN FRANCISCO, Dixie made a phone call and left a voicemail for Thomas. "George is taken care of. The sharks will find him before anybody else does. I'm heading to the hospital now. I should be finished with both of them as soon as the blonde comes to visit. Wait for me at the house. Then, we can get out of here." *At least, I'll get out of here.*

Pulling into the hospital parking ramp, she parked far away from any other cars, and climbed into the back of her rented SUV. Once there, she pulled off her latex gloves, changed out of her jeans and sweater, removed her wig and hat, and donned a nurse's uniform, complete with name tag, stethoscope, and cushioned, white shoes. Under the uniform she wore skin-tight leggings and a tank top.

Before leaving the car, she wiped down everything. Placing her jeans, sweater, shoes, wig, and hat in a garbage bag, she tossed it in the nearest dumpster and headed into the hospital. She knew she'd have to stay out of the main corridors in case someone asked who she was or what floor she worked on, but she had memorized the hospital layout, knew where the Intensive Care Unit was located, as well as restrooms and storage rooms close to it. The ICU was her goal.

She entered the elevator behind two other employees.

Chapter 68

ABOUT THE SAME time as Dixie was entering the hospital, Marta and the two agents were talking with one of the surgeons in a waiting room off the ICU.

"They are both very lucky people. The agent was fortunate he had on his vest. It's kind of odd the way the bullet hit both the vest and his arm. At first we thought it was two bullets, but that doesn't appear to be the case. He will be sore for a while, but will recover fine with therapy.

"As for the female victim, she had extensive wounds to her right side where the bullet did the most damage. We've repaired everything and luckily didn't have to remove her right lung. We'll have to see how she does in the next few hours, as those are the most critical with her type of wounds. As for the head wound, it looked a lot worse than it was. A bullet grazed her skull, leaving a trail of blood but not significant damage. We had to shave that part of her head to make sure we stitched everything back up. She'll have a headache, but most likely no significant neurological damage.

"Specialists in orthopedics, pulmonology, and neurosurgery were on the surgical team, so we have all the bases covered. Now, any questions?"

Marta spoke first. "When can we see them?"

"Not for at least another 12 hours. The female is heavily sedated and won't be coming out of it for several hours. The agent will probably start to come around in a couple of hours. I'd suggest you go home and come back in the morning. I will call you if there is any change."

Marta looked at Jon. "I really don't want to go home. I'd feel so helpless there."

"I hear you, but I think it's best if we do go and come back in the morning, Marta. No sense getting worn out here. Clark is on his way to San Francisco and should be arriving shortly." He looked at his watch. "Very shortly."

"Then, we need to call Ian and see what he's found. Clark can fill us on in the plan when he gets here. I really do think we should leave. Okay?"

After more questions and discussion with the surgeon, it was decided they would go back to Marta's. The surgeon promised he would keep them updated.

"Guys, I'm going to run to the restroom quickly before we go. I can meet you back here or by the car."

"We'll wait here for you. Take your time. I'll check on Clark's ETA."

"Great. I'll leave my bag here and be right back." Marta placed her bag on the chair next to Jon and headed down the hall to the restroom. A nurse walked in ahead of her and held the door for her. "Thank. . . ." That was all she managed to say before being grabbed from behind, whacked on the head, and her arms twisted around to her back. Marta was momentarily stunned, dizzy with the blow to the head, and tried to catch herself as she fell forward. Her knees threatened to buckle. She tried to focus.

"Don't make a sound, or your life will end right now." Marta could feel something cool and sharp pressing under her chin.

Trying to figure out what was going on, Marta caught a blurry glimpse in the mirror over the sink, and saw the nurse. Somewhere in her brain she tried to piece together why a nurse would be hurting her. She struggled slightly, and the sharp object pressed harder into her skin. "Don't move. Got it? You've messed up my life for the last time. I can make this quick and painless right here, or I can do this slowly. Your choice. But, you will die. Here. Today. Then I'm taking care of your friend."

Slowly, Marta realized what the nurse was holding under her chin, and she struggled as the adrenalin kicked in. *I can't panic.*

"I said, don't move." The nurse adjusted her hold on Marta.

Just then, Marta's phone, tucked in her pocket, rang, startling them both. Marta tried to take advantage of her attacker's momentary pause, but she was still somewhat dazed, and clumsy, and the nurse was too quick to react. The knife pressed harder, this time drawing blood.

"I see. You want to suffer. That's fine with me."

Marta's phone stopped ringing and then started again. This time, the nurse ignored it.

"Okay. That's it." She drew more blood as she started to slice across Marta's throat.

Marta was helpless as a few drops of blood fell onto the floor. *I can't die. Clark is coming.*

Chapter 69

THE RESTROOM DOOR flung open as two men, one crouched and one standing tall, weapons aimed at the nurse and Marta, filled the doorway. "Drop the knife." The tall man shouted, causing the nurse to jerk the knife deeper into Marta's skin. More blood spilled onto the floor, creating a small, dark red pool on the white tile. Marta felt herself go limp with pain as she sagged ever so slightly.

That was enough of an opening for the crouched man as he fired a single shot. The nurse, a bullet hole in her forehead, slumped to the floor, taking Marta with her. Blood flowed onto the tiled floor.

"Marta, can you hear me? Hang in there. Over here, doctor. She's bleeding badly." The taller man stayed standing with his weapon still pointed at the nurse. The crouched man stood up and gently moved Marta away from the nurse and toward the two doctors entering the restroom.

The nurse lay unmoving on the floor as the commotion surrounded her.

When Marta was loaded on a stretcher and whisked away, the two men put on gloves and knelt by the dead nurse. Hospital security joined them. "She has a name tag, but it's not an official hospital name tag. And, she doesn't have the right code on the back of it." One of the hospital guards remarked as he turned it over. "I wonder how she got to this floor. It's a secure floor."

"We'll let you figure out that part. We need to figure out if she's working alone or if someone else may be lurking around. We still have guards by ICU, right?" One of the men turned to the other one as he asked.

"Yeah, we do. No one's getting in there."

"Okay. Let's see what else she has, and then let's check out the security tapes. We'll have our guys process this room."

"Sounds good. We'll meet you in the control room."

"Jon, you're in charge here. I'm going to see how Marta is, and I'll meet you there in a little while."

Throughout the next hour Clark knew security had increased outside ICU. The hospital was carefully inspected in search of an accomplice, and fingerprints were sent to the forensics lab. He also knew he wanted to view those tapes. But, right now, it was more important to wait for the surgeon who had been taking care of Marta.

Chapter 70

IN ANOTHER PART of San Francisco, he paced, waiting for a phone call from Dixie telling him the blonde was dead. Plans were finalized for Dixie and him to head to London on tonight's British Airways flight from SFO, tickets sitting on his now empty desk. Glancing at them, he double-checked the departure time of five hours from now. He picked them up and placed them inside his jacket pocket with the passports.

His pacing resumed as it took him from his office to his large foyer where seven, priceless, original paintings had hung. From there, he moved to the gallery off the ballroom, where another four had hung. The walls looked bare, but he didn't really notice as he was already picturing them hanging in his estate north of London. His man in London would meet the plane and then have them moved from the airfreight terminal. They would all be there waiting for him when they arrived. He smiled in anticipation.

Walking back toward his office, his footsteps echoed in the almost empty house. "I'm glad this sold quickly. I can't wait to get out of here. It served its purpose."

He looked at his phone for the tenth time in 20 minutes and spoke into the space. "Damn. What's going on? Dixie doesn't miss, and she's never late. She should be on her way back here by now.

Her voicemail was over an hour ago. I think it's past time for me to show her who's boss."

Mumbling, he rubbed his temples, wishing the searing, pounding pain would go away. Then, he sat down, got back up, and started pacing again. His mind returned to the phone call he just received from Italy.

"I can't believe that idiot. Who drops their phone and then runs over it? More brawn than brains, that one. I could barely hear what he was saying. And, that part about not remembering where the apartment is. He's either losing it or trying to trick me, and I don't like it. And, he doesn't know what happened to Serge. What the hell's going on over there? Can't have loose ends like that. I think it's time they all disappeared. Don't need any of them anymore. I'd have Carlo take care of them, except I don't know what happened to that joker. He just disappeared, and I didn't have anything to do with that. If he was in jail, I'd know. It's ridiculous how those idiots can't even think for themselves.

"Well, too bad for Carlo's sake. I'll be gone from here, and he won't be able to find me, or call, or text me. As soon as we head to the airport, I'm ditching this phone. He's hanging himself out to dry.

"Now, where the hell is Dixie?"

No one answered his incoherent questions as he made one last trip through the house. "I need to leave pretty soon. She'll have to find her own way to the airport." Their large suitcases were sitting by the door.

Chapter 71

ALTERNATELY SITTING AND then pacing in the small waiting room by the surgical wing, Clark looked up when the door opened, and the surgeon walked in. Gesturing to the chairs, he sat down next to Clark.

"First, she's doing well. Since we were able to get her into surgery quickly, she didn't lose a lot of blood. It looked a lot worse than it actually was. Her carotid arteries were not damaged, and the knife didn't penetrate the skin very deeply. She had 27 stitches and will have some soreness, but shouldn't have much of a scar after a while. She also took quite a bump on the head. She'll be awake shortly, but not real coherent. Do you want to see her?"

"Absolutely. How long will she be in ICU or the hospital for that matter?" The two men headed out of the waiting room.

"She'll only be in ICU until she's awake and we check her vitals. Then, we'll move her to a room. I want to keep her for at least three days." They entered ICU.

Clark looked at her, with tubes in her arms and dark stitches circling much of her neck. He squeezed her hand, bent down, kissed her cheek, and told her he would be back.

"Doc, I need to see what the security tapes show and see what else is happening. Call me when she wakes up." The surgeon nodded as they left, and Clark headed to the security administrative office where he met up with Agent Hansen and the hospital security.

"We can see how she followed another employee into the hospital from the employee parking garage, and we've identified her car. It's being inspected as we speak. Her fingerprints are being run, and we found a phone in her pocket. I was just getting ready to call you, Clark. How's Marta?"

"She's out of surgery, but not awake. The surgeon told me she came through okay and no major damage. She was lucky. The doc is going to call me when she comes to. Now, let me fill you in on the plans. Or at least the plans up to this point." His phone rang, and he noticed it was Pete.

"Pete, Jon is here, too. Start over."

Chapter 72

"CLARK, YOU KNOW about the issues here in Italy, the murder of the alleged forger, and all of that. Well, we just had a run-in with a courier at the forger's home. Unfortunately, he's dead, but we used his phone to contact his boss. Or, at least we're pretty sure it's his boss. The first time, we couldn't complete the trace, but this time we got him.

"You're not going to believe it. He's in San Francisco, and we've got an address."

"Pete, hold on. Ian is on the other line. Can I call you back?"

"Sure. I'll be here."

Clark picked up the call from Ian. "Pete was just starting to tell me what's been developing. What's up?"

"Clark, Pete probably told you how they were able to trace a call to someone there in San Francisco. We don't know if he's the leader, or just another go-between, or what. But, it's a start. Special Agent Stephen Larch is the lead, and he has a team ready to go. They want you and Jon with them. Here's the address of the rendezvous point."

"Thanks, Ian. We'll head there now." Clark hung up, called Pete back to fill him in, and made a quick stop by ICU before he and Jon headed to the rendezvous point.

Special Agent Larch was discussing the plan with the team as Clark and Jon pulled up. "Clark, good to see you again. Here's the address of the caller. Hopefully, he's still there. We're not going in hot, as we don't want to spook him, in case he's not alone. This is the plan, and this is our backup in case he gets suspicious. How are things at the hospital with Greg and the lady who were shot?"

"Good to see you, too, Steve. They're both out of surgery and in recovery. Greg is doing better, and Suzie, the woman who was shot, is holding her own right now. It's kind of wait and see. You probably don't know about the other issue at the hospital, do you?"

"No. What's going on?"

Clark filled him in and when he was finished, Steve had questions. "Do you think that incident is somehow related to this issue and this caller?"

"I'd have to say yes, based on gut instinct. But, no firm evidence to go on."

The team of seven men left and headed out to complete the plan.

Chapter 73

IN HIS NEAR-EMPTY San Francisco mansion, he sent a text to Dixie. When she did not immediately answer, he looked at his watch. "Okay. That's it. I'm not waiting for her any longer. This is starting to smell bad. She's obviously run into something, or she would have let me know what's happening. I need to get going."

The next call he made was to the limousine driver, with instructions to pick him up in five minutes and deliver him and all the luggage to the SFO Airport. "I'll take her bags, but Dixie will just have to meet me in London if she misses this flight." Talking to his empty foyer, he moved all the bags closer to the door and looked around. "Time to get the hell out of here."

When the doorbell rang a couple of minutes later, he glanced out the foyer window and saw a black car sitting by the curb. Pulling the door wide open to let the driver in to pick up the six bags and take them to the car, he was completely caught off guard by the two men who muscled their way into his foyer.

"What the hell? Who are you?"

It quickly dawned on him neither of these men was his driver. That realization was followed by panic and a great desire to fight. Kicking and punching at the men, his adrenalin soared into high gear. Still, he was no match for the two well-trained thugs. One hit him on the side of his head with a metal bat, causing him to slump to the floor, while the other one put three well-placed shots into his upper body. He never felt a thing as he lay on the floor, his blood staining the gray and white marble tiled floor.

Nodding to each other, they left the foyer as quickly and quietly as they came.

One of them pulled out his phone and sent a text. "Mission accomplished. He's dead. See you in London."

He smiled to the other man as they got in their car and left.

$\mathcal{C}$hapter 74

SEVERAL MINUTES LATER, one black SUV pulled into the driveway of the mansion, two others parked around the corner. As planned, Special Agent Larch made his way to the front door, looking for security cameras that might tip off the owner. Seeing one, he pulled his cap down a little further on his head and walked up the flight of marble stairs toward the front door. The rest of the agents and Clark surrounded the stairs and the hidden garage door.

Special Agent Larch stopped, slightly lowered his chin, and spoke into his mic. "Something's wrong. The front door is ajar, and something's not right. Let's go in hot. NOW."

All men converged on the front door as Steve, standing to the side, opened it with his foot. It opened easily, revealing the bloody body lying on the floor.

"Call 911." Seeing no one in the foyer, he rushed to the body. Four other agents covered him and then made a sweep of the ground floor and upstairs. "Clear." All of the agents reported.

"No one else is here. But, the place is pretty well cleaned out. No furniture to speak of, no clothing, no personal items, nothing. Looks like he was leaving town." Jon looked at the bags sitting by the door.

Steve stood up. "An ambulance is not going to help him. There's no pulse. Someone didn't want him alive." As he stood up, he noticed the envelope inside his open jacket. With gloves on, he carefully removed it. "Two tickets to London. One way. Home address is listed in England. Well, I'll be. Look at these." He pulled two passports out of another pocket.

"Sir Antonio Furst and Lady Simone Smythe on the passports and the tickets. Huh. Clark, your mystery just became clearer. Or muddier."

Clark's phone rang about the time he was going to answer. "It's the hospital. Marta's awake. I'm heading there and will catch you guys later."

"Sounds good, Clark. We'll all debrief with a call to Ian in two hours. Meet us at the office. We need to talk to the local police and see what went on here."

Sirens stopped as an ambulance and three patrol cars pulled up outside.

"You go, Clark. I'll handle this."

Chapter 75

MARTA WAS SITTING up in bed with most of the tubes removed, except for one in her arm. Clark looked at her eyes and then her dark stitches surrounding much of her neck. "Oh my God, Marta. I thought I had lost you." Tears welled up in his eyes. "We really need to talk."

Trying to smile, tears ran down her cheeks as well. Swallowing was painful, talking almost impossible. The physician intervened. "Try not to talk, Marta. Use this pen and paper to communicate for right now. It will get better in a few hours.

"Clark, she's doing well. We're moving her to her own room now, and I'll keep her for at least three more days. She's on pain meds as she needs them. I wanted you to see her before we move her. Then, she needs to get some rest. Why don't you tell her good-bye and come back in a couple of hours?"

Clark nodded, squeezed her hand, and looked into her eyes. "I love you, Marta."

More tears in her eyes as she tried to swallow. Hastily and clumsily, she scribbled on the pad of paper. 'Love you.' Clark leaned over to kiss her forehead.

"Okay, Clark. Out of here. You can tell her later."

Clark smiled at her once more as he left the ICU.

Chapter 76

A FEW HOURS later, everyone was assembled. Ian and Pete were conferenced in, and Ian took the lead. "Okay, Steve, fill me in."

He went over the events as they knew them. Some details were still missing. "We aren't sure who killed him. No fingerprints anywhere and ballistics is still working on the bullets. They don't have a lot of hope, though.

"This is what we do know. Sir Antonio Furst and Thomas Smith were one in the same. We're not sure where the name Sir Antonio Furst comes from, but his real name is Thomas Smith, and he grew up outside of London. No royalty or anything in the family. He has quite the history, none of it good. Many, many years ago, he was questioned for his mother's murder, but there wasn't enough evidence to tie it to him. That one is still an unsolved crime. But, digging deeper, he was abused as a child, and I'd bet money he did her in.

"His mother owned a shop and an antique auction company in London. Quite successful, apparently, as she had a major collection of small paintings and other antiques. It seems he started making money by selling those items, some even before she was killed. There are reports and accusations from her on record with the London police. She would press charges and then drop them."

"Steve, how did she die?"

"Car bomb. One morning she left home, started her car, and it blew up when she started to drive away. Thomas claimed he was asleep and heard the bomb. But, the investigation revealed some questionable items in his room. He says they were for a science experiment, and no one could prove or disprove that. A witness came forward and said he saw Thomas around her car the night before. But, before that witness could testify or even be questioned further, he mysteriously disappeared. Haven't heard from him, and they never found him."

"Okay. Please continue, Steve."

"Like I said, he started selling a bunch of her stuff. There are various complaints from all over about some of the items being sold more than once, some of them being switched, and some being placed at illegal auctions. This is all documented with the local police in London.

"Then, it seems like he moved on to bigger and better items. More expensive. We're not sure when or where the forgeries came into the picture, but there are reports of sales of questionable art-work. Ian, you'll have to fill in those blanks with Interpol."

"Steve, we've already started. We also found possible ties to the murders here in France, and Pete was instrumental in getting information from Italy. It seems like his world was caving in quickly. That's probably why he was leaving there and heading to London. He may or may not have known everything that was happening. We'll probably never know the real story about all the forgeries. Now, what about the paintings there at his mansion?"

"Ian, the place is empty. Nothing at all here. I've already contacted the London police, their airport security, and customs. My guess is they're either already in London or coming in on a plane in the near future. He was definitely leaving here."

"Clark, thanks. By the way, how is Marta?"

"Out of surgery and getting better. I will head back to the hospital after I'm done here."

"Good. So, back to Thomas Smith. Steve, what else do you have?"

"Well, he had two passports in his pocket, and two tickets with the same names."

Clark's phone buzzed, and he excused himself and took the call.

$\mathcal{C}$hapter 77

"SORRY FOR THE interruption, but that was the local guys from the FBI. Their forensics team has identified the nurse from the hospital who tried to kill Marta. Her name is Dixie Smith. They found a small purse in her pocket with a passport and a ticket to London."

"She's wanted for a couple of murders. The FBI and Italian police have been looking for her." He shook his head. "Those two must have been quite the team."

"Right. We'll process that and talk to the local police and FBI. Why do you suppose she wanted Marta dead? Any ideas?"

"Well, Marta was the one who spotted a forgery in Milan, then had some issues at a gallery in Venice, and was involved with this Picasso forgery here. Not sure if that's enough to want her dead, but maybe she was another loose end. It seems like they had been tying up all sorts of loose ends recently. For all we know, this Dixie was supposed to kill Marta and then finish off Suzie, too."

"You're probably right, Clark. Does anybody have any idea who killed Thomas? Any idea how they got to him before us? Do we have a leak somewhere, or was it just simple timing?"

"No clue on any of those questions. There is a security camera outside his front door, but when we looked at the footage, all we can see are two big guys arriving 10 minutes before we do. They're wearing black, no faces showing, and the camera didn't catch their car. They're in the house for about three minutes and then calmly walk back out. We didn't find any cameras inside the house. And, that neighborhood doesn't have street cameras, so no luck on the car."

"Okay, for now. We're going to have to keep this as an open murder investigation. With any luck, we'll get it solved. Pete, you wrap up in Italy. Clark, let us know what the team in London finds with the paintings. Then, we'll have to authenticate those and return any originals. Steve, please wrap up San Francisco.

"Clark, give Marta a hug from me. For now, we're finished. We can all report back in at our meeting next week. Any questions?"

Everyone shook their head and said goodbye as Clark headed out the door to go back to the hospital.

"Clark, wait. The FBI just called. The dead woman's phone just received a text. They're using her fingerprint to unlock her phone and retrieve the message."

$\mathscr{E}$pilogue

TWO WEEKS LATER, Clark, Marta, Suzie, Pete, Greg, and Jon were all sitting in Marta's living room. Lady, with her head on Suzie's lap, sat next to her chair, and Shadow purred on Marta's lap as Clark held her hand. Her stitches had faded to a dark ring around her throat. There were a couple of empty bottles of champagne, and everyone had a glass. Ian had just arrived.

He accepted a glass as he looked at Suzie and her cropped hairstyle, with only a few stitches visible on one side. The bandages around her chest were covered by her sweater. "Glad you and Greg are both healing well. You look good with short hair, and we're all glad the bullet only grazed your head. We thought we may have lost both of you in that alley." Suzie smiled at him.

He took a long look at Marta and sighed. "Marta, you look remarkably good considering your brush with a knife. We all thought we had lost you for sure. Here's to keeping everyone safe now." He raised his glass in a toast. "Now, I'll fill you all in on what has happened in the last couple of weeks and what we have been able to piece together.

"Marta, it appears you were the intended target all along. Suzie just happened to get in the way, by being your friend." Suzie looked at Marta and smiled. "This all started with some events you were involved in or witnessed, Marta. These events, by themselves, really don't seem drastic enough for someone wanting to kill you, until you understand the people involved.

"First, you caused both Thomas and Dixie to lose paintings they really wanted to possess. Apparently, they were both so greedy and focused, they could only see one goal. And, you stood in their way. In their minds, you were the single reason they didn't have what they wanted. We learned much of how they worked from their assistant, who maintained their mansion outside of London.

"When we intercepted him at the airport, he had just picked up the paintings which were shipped from their home here in San Francisco. Probably those you both saw at the party. When we questioned him, we hit the jackpot. He started talking and hasn't stopped. He told us he had been working for Thomas for several years and was becoming more worried about Thomas' health in recent months.

"He felt sorry for Thomas. But, at the same time, Thomas worried him. He would fly off the handle and come up with all sorts of plans to get rid of someone. Sometimes, for no apparent reason. The assistant told us a story about Thomas wanting to kill the postman and bury him in the flower garden because the mail was 20 minutes late. Another time, Thomas became so paranoid about a museum clerk who he thought was watching him, he had his car blown up. Apparently, these actions were becoming more frequent.

"This might be due to the brain tumor they found when they did the autopsy. According to the M.E. this was a good sized tumor and in a place where rational thinking was being compromised. We'll never know for sure if that's why things escalated with him.

"The assistant remembers meeting Dixie about four years ago and never liked her. She wasn't your average thief and silent part-ner and he wasn't sure how they met. In the past couple of years Dixie had become more forceful, demanding, and devious, and he didn't like that. According to him, Thomas and Dixie were fighting more and more about who was in charge and who called the shots.

"In fact, the assistant in London was more scared of her than Thomas. For all we know, Thomas was afraid of her, too. Thomas would call himself the boss when she wasn't around. She'd get mad if she heard him say that; mad to the point of tormenting Thomas. He told us about a time he overheard Dixie talking to some huge guy at the mansion in London. They were discussing murders of people in France. He shuddered as he told us about their conversation. It seems torture was her M.O. and, according to the assistant, she enjoyed it. They were talking and laughing about car bombs, body parts, and all sorts of other acts. She even laughed when she told the guy what she wanted done to Thomas. The assistant really was afraid of her, especially lately.

"He and Dixie had a run-in about the way he was supposedly catering to Thomas' whims. She didn't like it, and she threatened him. In great detail, she told him how she would torture him and then end his life. Right after that, the assistant started keeping a journal with names, dates, and everything that bothered him. It's quite the treasure trove of information. He's cooperating with the authorities, and we've already linked Dixie to multiple murders, here and in Europe. These go back several years, even before she joined forces with Thomas.

"We are fairly certain she was the mastermind, not Thomas. Apparently, she hired the hit men and thugs, only after they performed a kill for her. But, she had Thomas make all the phone calls. She was covering her bases. When her thugs didn't perform up to her standards, she got rid of them and did the dirty work herself. Thomas took orders from her, according to the assistant.

"Remember the text her phone received after she was killed? The message said Thomas was dead and he or they would meet her in London, so for that reason we did not publically let any information out about her death. One of our guys then responded to that text, telling that person they would meet them at a specific pub the following day. When two unusually big guys entered the pub at the appointed time, we were there to meet them. Upon attempting to take them into custody, one of them pulled his weapon and was killed by one of our agents. The other one surrendered and is talking. His list of names coincides with the names the assistant gave us. And, he kept referring to Dixie as his boss. He told us they thought Thomas was just somebody who hung around Dixie. They didn't take orders from him. Who would have thought?

"As for the paintings, Pete assisted our lab guys in finding the key symbol the forger painted. The forger was brilliant, both in his painting and in locating that key so only the right people would find it. This now allows us to catalogue and return the originals to their owners. We'll destroy the forgeries.

"We should be able to wrap up most, if not all, of this in the next couple of weeks. Different law enforcement agencies will receive reports, enabling them to close several open murder investigations." He looked around the room.

"Any questions?"

Everyone sat, shaking their heads, and attempted to digest everything Ian had told them in the past hour. All had relieved smiles. Clark looked around at everyone.

"Ian, I think we're all reassured to know this is pretty much finished, and we can get on with our lives." He looked at Suzie. "Your shop is repaired, and as soon as you're ready, you can get back to business." She smiled as Lady gave a soft woof.

"That sounds great. Thanks."

"Pete, I'll see you later in the year in Paris."

"Will do, Clark."

Clark smiled as he looked at Marta and Shadow. "Marta and I are taking a much-needed, private vacation, and the rest of you can find some other criminals to chase." Clark put his arm around Marta as Shadow stood up and meowed.

About the Author

WENDY VANHATTEN IS a published author, editor-in-chief for "Prime Time Living Magazine," wine, food, and travel editor for "WEMagazine," and travel enthusiast. She has taught writing at the college level, writing workshops, and is affiliated with Bay Area Travel Writer Organization, http://www.batw.org/.

Her children's books, the *Max and Myron* series, teach children to read while developing good character traits.

Travel advice and photos are updated weekly on her blog at www.travelsandescapes.blogspot.com. Her books are available online at Amazon or from her website, www.wendyvanhatten.com.

Additional Titles by Wendy VanHatten

My Life, The Sequel: A Girlfriend's Guide to Personal Success

When the Cat Speaks . . . Listen: A purr . . . fectly good way to enjoy life

Dad's Hidden Box

HIDDEN TRUTHS SERIES

Champagne Lies
Vineyard Secrets
Dark Legacy
The Secret of the Purloined Bracelet

MAX & MYRON SERIES

by Wendy VanHatten and R David Kryder with illustrations by Corie Barloggi

　　Max and Myron Learn Please and Thank You Max and
　　Myron, My First Day of School
　　Max and Myron I'm Sorry, Please Forgive Me Max & Myron
　　Learn Please Don't Tease
　　Max & Myron Learn Big and Small, Short and Tall
The Authorship Journey: A profitable adventure? by Wendy Vanhatten, Ginger Marks, Misty Taggart, and Tracee Gleichner

Available on Amazon.com and fine bookstores everywhere.